The Old H

50 Ann

D1354759

William Trevor was born in Mitchelstown, Co. Cork, in 1928, the son of a bank official, and spent his childhood in provincial Ireland. He studied at Trinity College, Dublin. Working first as a sculptor and teacher, then as an advertising copywriter, he published his first novel in 1958.

His subsequent novels have won numerous prizes, including the Hawthornden Prize, the Heinemann Fiction Prize, and the Yorkshire Post Book of the Year Award. He is a three-times winner of the Whitbread Book of the Year Award, for The Children of Dynmouth (1976), Fools of Fortune (1983) and Felicia's Journey (1994), and has also been shortlisted four times for the Booker Prize, most recently for The Story of Lucy Gault in 2002. His latest novel is Love and Summer (2009).

William Trevor is also an acclaimed writer of short stories. His complete output was collected into two handsome volumes by Viking Penguin in 2009. In 1999 he was awarded the prestigious David Cohen Prize for a lifetime's literary achievement, and in 2002 he was knighted for his services to literature. He has lived in Devon for many years.

The Old Boys

WILLIAM TREVOR

PENGUIN BOOKS

PENGUIN BOOKS

Published by the Penguin Group
Penguin Books Ltd, 80 Strand, London WC2R 0RL, England
Penguin Group (USA) Inc., 375 Hudson Street, New York, New York 10014, USA
Penguin Group (Canada), 90 Eglinton Avenue East, Suite 700, Toronto, Ontario, Canada M4P 2Y3
(a division of Pearson Penguin Canada Inc.)
Penguin Ireland, 25 St Stephen's Green, Dublin 2, Ireland (a division of Penguin Books Ltd)
Penguin Group (Australia), 707 Collins Street, Melbourne, Victoria 3008, Australia
(a division of Pearson Australia Group Pty Ltd)
Penguin Books India Pvt Ltd, 11 Community Centre, Panchsheel Park, New Delhi – 110 017, India
Penguin Group (NZ), 67 Apollo Drive, Rosedale, Auckland 0632, New Zealand
(a division of Pearson New Zealand Ltd)
Penguin Books (South·Africa) (Pty) Ltd, Block D, Rosebank Office Park,
181 Jan Smuts Avenue, Parktown North, Gauteng 2193, South Africa

Penguin Books Ltd, Registered Offices: 80 Strand, London WC2R 0RL, England

www.penguin.com

First published by The Bodley Head 1964
Published in Penguin Books 1966
Reissued in this edition 2014
001

Copyright © William Trevor, 1964
All rights reserved

The moral right of the author has been asserted

Set in 11/13 pt Dante MT Std
Typeset by Jouve (UK), Milton Keynes
Printed in Great Britain by Clays Ltd, St Ives plc

ISBN: 978-0-241-96925-0

www.greenpenguin.co.uk

Penguin Books is committed to a sustainable
future for our business, our readers and our planet.
This book is made from Forest Stewardship
Council™ certified paper.

To Jane

The meeting was late in starting because Mr Turtle had trouble with the lift. Having arrived successfully at Gladstone House, he entered the lift, struck the button marked 5 and ascended. On the way he began to think, and his train of thought led him into the past and absorbed him. At the fifth floor Mr Turtle still thought; and when the lift was summoned from below he descended with it. A man in overalls opened the doors at the basement and Mr Turtle got out. 'Thank you, thank you,' he said to the man. 'Room three-o-five,' he said to himself; but all he could find was an enormous lavatory and a furnace-room. The concrete passages did not seem right to Mr Turtle, nor did the gloomy green and cream walls, the bare electric light bulbs and the smell of Jeyes' Fluid. 'I say,' Mr Turtle said to a woman who was mopping the floor, 'can you tell me where three-o-five is?' The woman didn't hear him. He repeated the question and she stared at him with suspicion.

'Three-o-five? Do you want Mr Morgan?'

'I think I'm a little lost actually. Actually I want room three-o-five.' The woman didn't know what Mr Turtle meant by room three-o-five. Her province was the basement.

'I'm sorry,' she said, mopping round Mr Turtle's feet. 'I don't know no room three-o-five.'

'I'll be late. I'm due at a meeting.'

'They didn't tell me about no meeting. You won't find no meeting in the basement, mister.'

Mr Turtle registered surprise.

'Is this the basement? I pressed the button for the fifth floor.'

So he went back to the lift, and when eventually he entered room three-o-five he was conscious of an angry glance or two: they didn't like one to be late. Mr Turtle began to make his excuses, retailing his conversation with the woman in the basement. Sir George Ponders, who was in the Chair, cut him off. The others nodded and shuffled. Mr Jaraby smiled.

The meeting was a routine one. The committee of the Old Boys' Association met a couple of times a year to discuss this and that and to survey the implementation of past proposals. The men around the table were of an age: somewhere between seventy and seventy-five. They served on the committee for two years, but one of them would be elected by the committee itself as next session's President. Thus there was a perpetual link. Part of the etiquette of the Association was that committee members were of the same generation and had been at the School at the same time. Another part was that there was never a committee of younger men; one's chance to serve came late in life.

Through the warm afternoon the voices droned in room three-o-five, agreeing and arguing. One man slept and snored, and was hastily woken. He blinked, jerking his limbs in confusion, protesting at the interruption and denying that he had fallen into a nap. They spoke of what they had been convened to speak about, interlacing business with reminiscence. 'Remember the day Burdeyon lost his monkey?' remarked Mr Sole. He smiled, his head to one side; speaking of the Headmaster of their day, an eccentric who had kept unusual pets. 'It had fleas,' Mr Cridley said. 'Burdeyon was a bit of an ass.' But Mr Jaraby, who had admired authority in his time, disagreed. A brief argument was pursued before Sir George called the meeting to order. Mr Swabey-Boyns, who had himself been responsible for the temporary disappearance of the monkey, voiced no comment.

The men's hands were spread before them on the table: hands with swollen veins, thin hands like pieces of stick, hands with shakes in them. One man's played with a pencil stub; another's drummed the hard surface without rhythm.

In deference to the heat the windows were open to their fullest extent, and a small fan buzzed and swivelled in a corner. There was a noise of traffic in the room, and the smell of dry city air.

2

Mr Turtle remembered the powdery roads of Gloucestershire in his childhood, a long time ago now. He remembered travelling in a dog-cart, slowly, through a day like this one. From Moreton to Evenlode, to Adlestrop and Daylesford. He and Topham minor stopping off to buy sherbet in Chipping Norton. And showing Topham the Slaughters and the Swells.

'No doubt we shall all meet soon again,' said Sir George Ponders. 'O.B. Day at the School at the end of the month. But I would remind you that when next we meet officially, at our final Dinner in September, we shall be voting for next year's President. As you know, Jaraby has been proposed.'

Mr Jaraby glanced quickly from face to face. Ponders. Sole. Cridley. Swabey-Boyns. Sanctuary. Turtle. Nox. Unless one of them produced a reason against it, he would automatically be elected. He caught Mr Nox's eye and felt a little jump in his stomach.

'I find it oppressive in here,' said Mr Swabey-Boyns. 'Have we reached the end of business?'

They took their leave of one another, shaking hands and murmuring.

On the way home Mr Jaraby bought two pounds of beetroot. He had remembered to bring his string bag, folded neatly in his pocket. As he watched the girl transferring the vegetable from the weighing-machine to his bag he thought about Mr Turtle. The man had been fifteen minutes late and had then attempted to waste further time by breaking into some story about a washerwoman. Really, the old fellow was beyond it. It was remarkable how some aged more rapidly than others: Turtle had been his junior at school, he was probably two years younger. He questioned the price of the beetroot and, as he always did, offered the girl less money than she demanded.

'I am delighted to hear it,' said Mrs Jaraby, in reply to some statement of her husband's about the meeting.

Mr Jaraby poured himself tea, moving his teeth about with his tongue. Food was wedged somewhere. When he had released it he said:

'You are not. You say you are delighted but in fact you take no interest in the matter at all.'

Mrs Jaraby watched her husband's cat stalking a bird in the garden. The room they sat in smelt of the cat. Its hairs clung to the cushions. The surface of a small table had been savaged by its claws.

'I was being civil,' said Mrs Jaraby.

'Turtle came in late. He kept us cooling our heels. He claimed to have been in the company of a charwoman.'

'Well, well.' She believed he kept the cat only because she disliked it. Once a week he cooked fish for it in the kitchen, and she was forced on that day to leave the house and go to a cinema.

'He seems twice his years. And I thought was looking remarkably unhealthy. He has a dicky heart, poor fellow.'

'Which one seemed twice his years? It is something I would like to see. He would be a hundred and forty.'

'Be careful now: you are deliberately provoking me.'

'I am merely curious. How does this ancient look? Is he withered like a dead leaf, crooked and crackling?'

'You are picking up my remarks and trying to make a nonsense out of them. Are you unwell that you behave in this way? Don't say we are going to have illness in the house.'

'I am less well than I would be if the cat were not here. Your Monmouth has just disembowelled a bird on the lawn.'

'Ha, ha. So now you claim illness because we keep a pet. Are you psychic that you know what happens on the lawn?'

'A normal pet I might welcome. But a cat the size of a tiger I draw the line at. I know what happens on the lawn because I can observe the lawn through the window from where I sit.'

'My dear woman, you are too clever by half. I have said it before and I can only repeat it.' Mr Jaraby took a long draught of tea and leaned back in his armchair, pleased that once again he had established the truth of his wife's contrariness.

In the garden the cat fluffed through the sticky feathers, seeking a last mouthful. The late evening sun cooled the glow of antirrhinums and delphiniums, and bronzed the stones of the

4

tiny rockery. The cat strode to the centre of the grass, its body slung high on black rods of legs, its huge furry tail extended in line with its back. A rat had once leapt at its left eye and bitten it from its head: there remained only a dark shell, a gap like a cave, with a hint of redness about it.

Mr Jaraby closed his eyes. He did not see how his election as President could now be vetoed. He felt agreeably warm, snug within his body. 'I want you to be Head of the House,' Dowse had said, and Jaraby had watched a dribble of saliva slip down a crevice at the side of his mouth. He had never forgotten that dribble of saliva, perhaps because the moment was an emotional one and details were important. Then, too, he had felt agreeably warm, as though the flow of pride heated his blood. Dowse had been old then, the droop of his head between his shoulders more noticeable every day. But in his time, in his prime, he had been the Housemaster of the century. In canvas shoes he had kicked a rugby ball over the bar from the half-way line. Some boy had once protested that Dowse had a privileged position; that he, the boy, could not retaliate to Dowse's thrashing; that the relationship between master and boy was no relationship at all, since the master ordered and the boy obeyed. So Dowse, having thrashed him once and listened, thrashed him again, in fair fight with the gloves on, with all the House as audience. Ever since his day the House had been known as Dowse's; few people remembered that once it had been otherwise. 'I want you, Jaraby, because you are the best man I have.' And Jaraby had remained with him in his room, listening carefully, drinking a glass of mild beer; while Dowse explained to him how to go about a beating. Jaraby felt privileged, for Dowse could still beat like no one else. He had that reputation, and had in the past proved it to Jaraby himself.

'When Dowse died,' said Mr Jaraby, 'I cried.'

Mrs Jaraby, who had taken up her knitting, said nothing.

'It was my last day but one. I had been Head of his House, I had served him well. And then, in all the excitements, in all the comings and goings, the trunks being fetched from the attics and

5

packed, the books returned, the cupboards cleared, I heard of his death. The Headmaster told me himself, since my position demanded that I be the first boy to hear. He summoned me and darkened the room by pulling the curtains. I remember it was a clear day in July. The sun scorched through the study windows and I remember being blinded for a moment when the curtains cut it away.'

'Death is a subject one can go on about –'

'Go on about? I am not going on about it. I am not being morbid. I am simply sharing with you the passing of a man who influenced me.'

'I do not mean that. I mean that death begets death. You have told me before of your Housemaster's death. Indeed, as I recall, you did so at our first meeting. No, I was just thinking that death is in the air.'

'My God, what do you mean by that?'

Mrs Jaraby was a thin, angular woman, very tall and of a faded prettiness. She possessed no philosophy of life and considered her use in the world to be slight. She had grown sharp through living for forty years with her husband. With another man, she often thought, she might well have run to fat.

'I mean nothing sensational, only what the words more or less state. We have reached the dying age. You speak of your friend Mr Turtle who is closer, you imply, to death than he is to life; whose heart does not stand up to the years. You take it all for granted. Your cat marauds and murders, yet you do not bother; for death is second nature to you.'

'Why, good God, is death second nature to me?'

'One gets more used to death as death approaches.'

'You are talking a lot of foolish poppycock.'

'Poppycock is foolish as it is. There is no need to embellish the word. I am saying what runs through my mind, as you do.'

'You are picking up my words again. I was perfectly happy when I entered this room. I had met old friends and passed an agreeable afternoon. Yet thoughtlessly you sought to disturb me.

You talk of a murder in our garden when only a humble cat follows the dictates of his nature. The cat must find his prey, you know.'

'Your cat is fed and cared for. He is not some wild jungle beast and should not behave as such. I sometimes think that Monmouth is not the usual domestic thing and might interest people at a zoo. Have you thought of trying the animal at a zoo?'

'I fear for your sanity. You are a stupid woman and recently you have developed this insolence. Most of what you say makes little sense.'

'A moment ago you called me too clever by half. I was simply trying to make communication, to stimulate a conversation. Is there any harm in that?'

'You have not answered my challenge. I said you deliberately made me unhappy and nervous. I wished only to remind you of the death of Dowse, and yet no sooner had I spoken than you turned his passing into evidence of universal decay and death. Half the time I do not understand a word you say.'

'We are seventy-two, you must remember that. Communication is now an effort. It is not the easy thing that younger people know.'

'You sit there knitting and going on. You say you see my cat become a monster in the garden. We are in the English suburbs, foolish lady; half a world away from Africa. You say this and that and anything that suddenly occurs to you. Does it not also occur to you that your idleness will mean dinner is an hour or so late? I bought two pounds of beetroot. It awaits your attention on the kitchen table.'

'Dinner is cold and shall not be late. You may have it now if you wish. And why could I not have bought the beetroot? I am capable.'

Mr Jaraby laughed. 'I beg to contradict that. You are not capable of handling the purchase of this particular vegetable. Now, let me tell you. You will not for instance order that a beet be split before your eyes to prove its quality. You will not see that the split

7

beet comes from the same basket as the beets they give you. You are not interested in food. You will eat anything.'

'On the contrary. I will not eat tripe. Or calf's head. Or roe from a herring. Or blancmange. Or rice as a pudding. Or that powdered coffee you bring into the house –'

'You have had no hard times. I learnt as a boy to eat all that was put before me.'

'I have had no hard times. Nor have you. You have led a sheltered life. You are more finicky than I over food.'

Mr Jaraby's head drooped, for he wished to sleep. There was silence in the room for a moment. Then Mrs Jaraby said:

'It is time that Basil was back with us.'

Mr Jaraby slept. His head rolled on to his chest, his arms hung listless over the sides of his armchair. His wife poked him with a knitting-needle.

'I said it was time Basil was back with us.'

Mr Jaraby blew his nose and passed his handkerchief over his face to conceal his anger. He roared incomprehensibly. Then he said:

'I will not hear the name in this house. Nor will I see the man. Nor shall I tolerate him anywhere near me.'

'He needs our care.'

'He needs no such thing. He is wicked, ungrateful and intolerable.'

'You must come round to the idea. You cannot escape so easily.'

'I must do nothing. I am not obliged to come round to any idea. I have other matters on my mind, and shall see to them immediately.' He rose and crossed to his bureau. He opened it and slung down the top with some violence. He had seen it in Nox's eyes that Nox would make a fight of it. He could count on the others, but somewhere in his mind there was a pricking fear that Nox would not let him easily win.

'I dusted Basil's room today,' Mrs Jaraby said. 'It is comfortable and ready.'

She picked up the tea-tray and left the room.

On the morning of 20 September 1907, George Nox, then thirteen, stood in the study of the man who was about to become his Housemaster: H. L. Dowse, one-time reserve for a Welsh international rugby team, now of advanced years. Nox – for when he had stepped on to the train at Euston he lost all other identity – had heard before of H. L. Dowse. At his prep school the stories of Dowse's prowess on the sport fields had been widely quoted; as had his scathing tongue and the kind of stories that Dowse would tell you if he knew and liked you well. Nox had not quite known what to expect. He had thought of a younger man, because most of what he had heard about H. L. Dowse was concerned with the vigour of youth, or at least the prime of life. Yet the man who spoke to him now was bent and seemed almost a cripple. His back was narrow and hunched, his mouth had slipped far back into his face: beneath the greying, heavy moustache it seemed lipless and half sewn up. The voice was small and harsh, as though it travelled a long way, losing impetus on the way. 'You are Nox,' said this voice, and the deep dark eyes scanned a list to confirm the fact. 'Well, Nox, you are to begin a new life. You will spend here days that you will cherish all your life. You will look back on them with affection and, I trust, pride. I myself have not forgotten my schooldays. They were spent at this school too, so even at this early stage we have that much in common. Have you questions?'

Nox shook his head, but Mr Dowse insisted on hearing his voice.

'No, sir,' Nox said.

'You know why you are here, Nox?'

Nox paused in his reply. He had learnt already that it was not a good thing to know too much; though an equally poor impression was created by total ignorance.

'I am here to learn, sir.'

'Not only that, Nox. You might learn anywhere. You might explore the mind of Horace and Virgil in the seclusion of your home. You might be taught the laws of trigonometry by a man who daily visited you. No, Nox, you are here for more than learning. You will absorb knowledge, certainly. At least I hope you will: we cannot send you into the world an ignoramus.' At this Mr Dowse cackled with laughter that was not reflected in his face. He sniffed, and twitched his moustache this way and that. He was silent: Nox thought the peroration was over. He wondered about slipping away and leaving Mr Dowse to his many tasks. He shifted his feet and the Housemaster looked up sharply.

'What is the matter, boy?' Nox thought he looked like some animal he had seen in an encyclopedia, and tried for a moment to establish its name in his mind.

'Nothing is the matter, sir.'

'Then do not display impatience. You are treating me to a discourtesy. Do you understand the meaning of that word?'

'Yes, sir.'

'Good, good. When you leave this school that word shall never be allied with your name. Are you pleased by what I say?'

'Yes, sir.'

'You are about to receive, Nox, the finest form of education in the world. You will learn to live in harmony with your fellows, to give and to take in equal proportions. You will recognize superiority in others and bow to it. You will discover your place, your size, the extent of your self. You follow me? You will find that our school is the world in miniature; and your days here are a rehearsal for your time in that world. You are a privileged person to be allowed such a rehearsal. It means that when you leave here you leave with the advantage of knowing what lies beyond. You must make the most of your advantage. You must apply to the world the laws that apply to this school. You must abide by those rules; and you must see to it that others do the same. In life you will be one of the ones who lead the way; it is expected of you and you must fail neither yourself nor the School. So you see there is more to it all than mere mathematics and Latin. You will learn to take punishment and maybe in time distribute it. You will learn to win and to lose, to smile on misfortune with the same equanimity as you smile on triumph. The goodness that is in you will be carried to the surface and fanned to a flame, the evil will be faced fairly and squarely: you will recognize it and make your peace with it. We shall display the chinks in your armour and you will learn how best to defend yourself. When you are my age, Nox, I hope you will look back and know that we have made a good job of you. That is perhaps a facetious way of putting it, but remember that a touch of humour here and there is not out of place.'

'Yes, sir.'

'I would warn you against many things. I would warn you against playing the buffoon. I would warn you against furtive, underhand ways. Steer a straight course, know what you desire, speak up and look people in the face. Never abuse your body, it leads to madness. You know of what I speak?'

'I think so, sir.'

'Be direct, Nox. If you know, say so. If you do not, seek information.'

'I know what you mean, sir.'

'If already you have developed the habit, you will promise me to break it. It is the only promise I wish to extract from you. On all other matters there is mutual trust between us.'

'I promise, sir.'

'Good boy. Stand straight, head high, shoulders back. What are your games?'

'I am not good at games, sir.'

'That, you know, is not for you to say. We shall discover in our time what games you are good at. Did you play on a team at your preparatory school? Which games do you prefer?'

'I was not on a team, sir. I'm afraid, sir, I like no games at all.'

'I am sorry to hear that, Nox. That does not sound good. And I do not quite believe it: there was one game surely that above all the others you enjoyed?'

'No, sir.'

'You are trying me a little, you know. I have other boys to see, much to do. Did you never enjoy an afternoon's cricket?'

'No, sir.'

'Why did you not?'

'I think I was bored, sir.'

'So ball and bat bored you. Are they in some way beneath your contempt? Have you some notion in your head that you are cut out for better things? What are your hobbies?'

'Reading, sir. And stamps.'

'Indoor hobbies, Nox. You note that these are indoor activities? God has given us fresh air. He does not intend us to ignore it. Develop a healthy interest in some outdoor sport. I shall watch your progress. I see you as scrum-half for the School.'

Nox was a little frightened. He knew it was extremely unlikely that he would play scrum-half for the School or anywhere else. And the words *it leads to madness* had distressed and alarmed him.

'I shall place you in the care of the Head of the House. He is a fine, decent person and has your interest at heart as I have. He and his prefects are your masters. They demand and shall receive obedience. You understand me, boy?' The voice was suddenly stern, and Nox nodded, answering that he understood. Mr Dowse pressed a bell and sent a maid to fetch the boy he spoke of.

When he entered, Nox was immediately impressed by his size. He was bigger than Mr Dowse, with a square fleshy jaw, recently shaved, and short dark hair like bristles all over his head. He stood with his legs apart and his arms hanging loosely by his sides, and Nox was reminded of the Physical Instructor at his prep school.

'Come to my room,' this boy said when they were outside the Housemaster's study. They walked in silence through the strange passages, Nox a little behind his senior to accord him the respect that Mr Dowse had said was his due. The passages were panelled in smoky wood, which displayed in a long continuous line a series of photographs of teams.

'I am Head of the House,' the tall boy said when they were in his room. 'My name is Jaraby. This is where I live. You will fag for me with the other new boys in the House. All new boys fag for the Head of the House to begin with. It is so that I can keep an eye on you. Please report here at six sharp.'

Every day Nox blacked Jaraby's boots, tidied his books and helped to wash up the dishes from which Jaraby had eaten. At the end of the period, when the new fags were allocated to new masters, Jaraby kept Nox on as his own particular servant. It was not that he had taken a fancy to him; it was that he had not yet trained him to his satisfaction.

'You are slack, idle, slapdash and irresponsible,' Jaraby said. 'You shall remain with me until such time as you have mended your ways.'

Jaraby, who was a stickler for detail and discipline, was determined that Nox should do what was required of him; quietly, contentedly, and with the minimum of nonsense.

At nights in the long cold dormitory, anonymous beneath his blankets, Nox wept before he slept, and when he awoke his face was stiff with the dried salt of his tears.

Nox did not see much of his Housemaster. Twice a day he appeared in Chapel, his face jolting in time to the hymns; and occasionally, with Jaraby on one side of him and another prefect on the other, he would walk, muffled against the weather, away from the School and into the country. Nox wondered if his turn would ever come to accompany Mr Dowse on these rambles and, if so, what topics of conversation would be explored. Rumour had it that the Housemaster's companions reported to him their suspicions of junior boys abusing their bodies, and discussed how best to prove the facts and penalize the offenders. Laughingly, these junior boys repeated the grisly story that Mr Dowse had once castrated a lad in his study. New boys, green from their prep schools, believed it.

Despite Mr Dowse's prognostications, Nox did not shine at games. Jaraby put him down as a second-row forward in rugby practices, but his slightness of build was little help in the scrums and he often found himself, cradling his head in terror, beneath a collapsed formation of heavy limbs and flaying boots. He had a horror of the muddy ellipsoid and avoided it as best he could. Once, finding it unexpectedly in his hands, he started to run in the specified direction but was promptly brought down and the ball sank deep into his stomach, winding him and in fact cracking a rib.

'You are not much on the rugger field,' Jaraby said. 'Men in this House are expected to do a little better.' Jaraby's small eyes bored into his, and Nox felt himself accused of a crime. Jaraby was sitting idle at his table, playing with the nib of a pen. It was, Nox felt, a dangerous moment.

'I am off rugger at present. I broke a rib.'

'Why did you do that? You cannot expect just to break a rib and then be excused your games. This looks like slyness to me.'

'I broke it playing rugger. I fell on the ball.'

'You fell on the ball! Heavens, man, you are not expected to stumble about like a grandfather on the field.'

'I was tackled. I was running for the line.'

Jaraby threw down the nib and made a beckoning gesture with his head. When Nox approached he seized him by a scrap of hair on the nape of his neck. He looked at the squirming form with distaste.

'Make no mistake, Nox, I am up to your tricks. You are off games, you say. You cannot lend your illustrious presence to the rugby football field. Right. But at least you can go on a run. A broken rib will hardly prevent you from taking this mild form of cross-country exercise, eh? Come, Nox: remember, you know best. Well?'

'I'd better ask Matron, Jaraby.'

'Ask Matron! And write home to Mother while you're at it. Yes or no, Nox – it is your decision. Ask our Housemaster, he will tell you you must learn to take decisions. Shall I send you to ask Mr Dowse? It is no trouble, Nox; I shall be pleased to help you.'

'I will go on the run, Jaraby.'

'Two-thirty, tomorrow. Sharp.'

During his first months as Jaraby's fag Nox learnt to accept his fate with philosophy. Other boys were fags for less exacting prefects; and quite often happy, if dubious, relationships were formed. It was recognized that Nox had been unlucky; for somehow the prickly Jaraby seemed uninterested in relationships for their own sake, and certainly did not consider that his small, grubby fag was worthy of more attention than the efficient running of his study warranted. In Nox's new life Jaraby was everywhere. It was not the mere fact of receiving a *gamma* for a piece of English prose that distressed Nox; it was what Jaraby would say to him when Jaraby got to know about it. For somehow Jaraby always did seem to get to know. He knew everything that went on in the House and everything that concerned the boys who belonged to it. What Nox did, on the games field or in class, was inevitably 'not good enough'. Now and again in Chapel Nox felt the peering eyes of Jaraby upon him; and as he later collected mugs and plates for washing, Jaraby might question him about the effort he put into his singing. 'You must open your mouth wider, young Nox. When you sing you should display your lower teeth.' And Jaraby remembered that. He remembered telling Nox about showing his lower teeth and recalled the image of his fag standing on the hearth-rug, rolling down his lower lip to show what he could do. Weeks later Jaraby suddenly said: 'Well, Nox, are you practising your singing? Have you made progress? Let's see now – give us a verse of *Hills of the North*.' Shame and awkwardness made Nox feel light in the head. He couldn't sing at all. His treble voice was just an absurd quaver. His face reddened and he clutched at the first straw he thought of. 'I don't know the words, Jaraby.' But he knew it was too late; he knew that Jaraby had made a discovery that was easy to exploit. He took from him the hymn-book, and, glancing at the faces of Jaraby and his friends, he saw that their current expressions were neither kind nor unkind. In some odd way he felt it was their very neutrality that brought on the mounting tears behind his eyes. He thought they would be pleased if he succeeded, but he knew he would fail. 'Hills of the North, rejoice; river and mountain-spring, hark to the advent voice –' Jaraby held up a hand. 'You must show your lower teeth, man. Mouth open, lip well down. That's it. Try again.' But his voice was ridiculous now, with his face twisted like that, and they all laughed and then forgot he was there. On occasions like this, Nox even in the midst of his misery was aware that this was Jaraby's way of fulfilling his position: Nox was in his care, he was determined that Nox should eventually pass out of it a better person. Jaraby was doing his duty. Had Nox turned round on him and said: 'You are injuring me,' he would have thought that Nox was mad.

Cross-country running was dreaded by everyone. There were ditches full of cold, dirty water to negotiate. There was heavy mud that one had to scrape from time to time off the bottoms of one's shoes. And there was a time limit. If one dawdled and did not turn up where one should be at the prescribed hour, the prefects who waited there, ticking off names, would have gone. They came and went by road, on bicycles. If they left with names unticked on their lists it was assumed that the boys they belonged to had not taken part in the run at all. To have tramped and panted over five miles of uninviting countryside and then failed to arrive meant six strokes later that evening. The time limit was the most heart-breaking thing about the run.

Out of thirty or so boys who were listed there were nearly always two or three who didn't even start. They preferred to spend the afternoon reading in the lavatory and to take their punishment in time. They knew, in any case, that it was beyond the strength of their bodies to cover the ground in the allotted time. Nox was not one of these. He had failed before, but once or twice he had succeeded: he reckoned he stood a fifty-fifty chance. As he crossed the last ditch he could see Jaraby and two others standing at the top of the hill by the final stile. The pale afternoon sun glinted on the metal of their bicycles. Their laughter and voices carried easily in the clear air.

'Hurry, hurry,' one of the boys in front of him said to his companion. 'There's someone horrible behind us.' He said it because Nox was a new boy and a junior, an unknown quantity, unproved and mysterious. But Nox took the words at the value they stood for, and wondered why he should seem horrible to anyone.

Jaraby and his friends carried umbrellas, with which they struck the buttocks of the runners as they crossed the stile. Nox felt the sharp sting on his legs, and paused for a moment to catch his breath. He looked down the hill, across the ploughed land he had covered, and saw in the distance a couple of straggling wretches who had long since given up and were probably already crying in anger at the prospect of punishment. The senior boys mounted their bicycles, and Jaraby flung him his umbrella to carry. He nodded as he did so and said, surprisingly: 'Well done, Nox.' In the cold, darkening afternoon as he ran back to the school, Nox felt happy.

That night in bed Nox knew that there was something the matter with him. There was a pain in his chest just above the broken rib, and he guessed that in some way he had injured it. The next day the doctor explained that the rib had punctured his lung, and ordered him immediately to the sanatorium.

'You shouldn't have gone on that run,' Mr Dowse said, staring at him in the narrow iron bed. 'You were off games, Nox. Categorically so, Matron says. Yet you disobeyed her order. Now, Nox, I wish to hear why.'

'I did not think, sir –'

'No, you did not think. You did not think that you might do yourself a mischief. Are you so devoted to cross-country running? It surprises me that you are. For Jaraby says your performance is mediocre.'

'Jaraby was pleased, sir. I reached the stile in time. Jaraby was anxious that I should have exercise and fresh air. He thought it bad for me to hang about –'

'Hang about? Stiles? Why are you talking to me about stiles?'

'I am expl—'

'I know nothing of such things. If you had a complaint about Matron's decision you should have said so at the time, not go running to Jaraby for favours.'

Nox said nothing, and was carried away for a moment or two in an examination of Mr Dowse's mouth. He had never seen so slight a mouth on a human face before.

'Well, well?' snapped Mr Dowse.

'Well, sir –'

'Nox, it strikes me you do not understand much of what I say. It grieves me that you show so little initiative. I have much to do, much to see to. I cannot spend all my time with one recalcitrant boy.'

'I'm sorry, sir.'

Mr Dowse sighed and began to walk away. He glanced without interest at the other boys in the room. Then he returned to Nox's bed. 'You are not abusing yourself, boy?'

'No, sir.'

It was the first time since their initial meeting that Mr Dowse had conversed with him. He had a feeling that his stock was not high with the man, and hoped that with Jaraby it had risen since the day of the run, even though Jaraby had reported that his cross-country performances were mediocre.

'Nox, I want to see you.' Nox, on his way back to the School from the sanatorium, carried his belongings tied together, as tradition demanded, in his rug.

'You have been blabbing to Dowse.' Jaraby was frowning, his eyes lost in folds of flesh. He pointed a finger at Nox's chest and Nox knew that the accusation was important. 'Contradict me,' Jaraby went on, 'if I am wrong. The facts I have are that you stated I countermanded Matron's orders and put you down for a run. That is not true, now is it? You went voluntarily. You took the decision in this room yourself. Do you recall our conversation, Nox?'

'Yes, Jaraby.'

'So you told a lie. You placed the blame on me. There is no room in this House for liars. And that is something you must learn the hard way. Bend over, Nox.'

Jaraby beat him, and to Nox there seemed to be savagery in the strokes. They were six, slow, well-delivered strokes, and Nox felt sick as the last one fell. He had become used to the easy life of the sanatorium. He had become used to spending the day as he liked to: reading and looking through his stamps. The maids had chatted to him and fussed over him a bit; it was almost like home again.

Jaraby returned the cane to its place on the wall and told him to stand up. He did so, gathering the bundle from the floor. He saw that Jaraby's face was a little flushed, and he felt himself shivering with pain and hatred.

3

Mr Sole and Mr Cridley lived at the Rimini Hotel in Wimbledon. They had done so ever since Mr Sole's wife died two and a half years ago. It was a quiet, somewhat cheerless place, with an automatic telephone in the hall and the smell of boiling meat almost everywhere. It catered specifically for the elderly, and in spite of the implications of its title was little more than a boarding house. Miss Burdock, who ran it, was a brisk middle-aged woman with a massive bosom and a penchant for long grey clothes. Once a year, in June, she put on a flowered dress and went somewhere in the afternoon. She wore a hat on this occasion, a large white one with decorations on it, that had been handed down from her mother. She smeared a pale lipstick on her mouth and dyed the hairs on her upper lip. Her guests wondered where she went, but they never asked her. They preferred to conjecture, and they looked forward quite a lot to this special day. An old lady, now dead, had claimed to have seen Miss Burdock stagger as she returned after one of these outings, and had sworn there was alcohol on Miss Burdock's breath.

'The man has written about the washing machine,' Mr Sole said, passing to Mr Cridley a typewritten letter and a coloured leaflet. They were sitting in the sun-lounge after breakfast, going through their mail. In the sun-lounge there were wicker chairs and top-heavy plants in pots. There were small tables laden with photographs of relatives of long deceased guests, and shells and trinkets that had been left to Miss Burdock in various wills. An old wireless stood silent in a corner. It would crackle to life at five to ten when Miss Edge and Major Torrill and Mrs Brown in her wheelchair came to hear *A story, a hymn and a prayer*.

'Tasteless breakfast,' Mr Cridley remarked, perusing the letter about the washing machine. 'You can't cook fried eggs like that. This fellow says he'll give you a demonstration. I'd take him up on that.'

A clock, set in a pleated gilt shape that might have suggested a fan if the clock had not been added, chimed from the wall. It was nine o'clock. The dining-room would be cleared by now: early to rise was the order of the day at the Rimini.

'I'm in doubt,' said Mr Sole. 'I don't know that I quite like the sound of this fellow. Does the letter strike you as being a bit pushing? And I do not understand the expression *your dealer*. I have no dealer; I do not even know one. The advertisement did not mention dealers.'

'The dealer will give you a demonstration, or, failing that, the chap who wrote the letter will. He says so. "I should be pleased . . . at your convenience . . . et cetera, et cetera." I wouldn't say pushing, you know. Seems a decent sort of fellow to me.'

The two men, who for more than sixty years had never been very much out of touch, were quite similar in appearance: spare of form, with beaky, weathered faces and strands of whitening hair. By strangers they were often taken for brothers. Of the two, Mr Cridley was the tetchier, though his tetchiness came only in flashes and was a sign of his age, for in earlier days he had been the more temperate. Age had calmed Mr Sole and emphasized what had always been true; that Mr Cridley led and Mr Sole followed.

'It is not at all explicit,' said Mr Sole. 'He does not say if he will come and give a demonstration here. I think he means we must travel to him or to this dealer you speak of. That will not do. I fear we must write this off.'

'I have heard from the central heating people. It seems quite a good system they offer, and their brochure is most colourful.'

'Is there a personal letter?'

'Yes, and agreeably written. The telephone number has sixteen lines. They must be in a big way.'

'The heating people I wrote to said I should have sent money.

I remember they did not even enclose a leaflet. I call that bad business.'

'People expect a leaflet if there is a coupon. It is a waste of a stamp otherwise. I told you to be wary. It was a very small advertisement.'

'Listen to this: *Smokers delight in using Eucryl smokers' tooth-powder, it removes unsightly tobacco film instantly makes teeth white again.* And then it says: *Without any fag at all!*'

'I don't understand it. Is it a letter?'

'It's in the newspaper. It is only difficult to understand because of economy with punctuation. You often complain of nicotine on your teeth.'

'Is there a coupon?'

'No. It just says: *Buy a two-bob tin of smokers' tooth-powder and prove it for yourself.*'

'One should not be asked to prove anything for oneself. Proving should be seen to by the manufacturers.'

'Do you recall,' said Mr Sole, tired for the moment of the subject, 'those chain letters that used to fascinate us so? You copied a letter six or eight times and forwarded half a crown to a specified stranger –'

'To the name at the top of the list.'

'And it was very bad luck to break the chain. One was warned against that.'

'An insidious business, those chains. Based on compulsion and fear. Someone may have made a lot of money.'

'A chain of which I was an ardent link was begun by a British major in the Boer War. The man was dead, the letter claimed, and if I'm not mistaken there was talk of his having begun the chain as he lay expiring on the battlefield, the implication being that one insulted a soldier's memory if one did not play the required part.'

'There was a chain letter that got going at school. Burdeyon spoke of it. He likened it to current crime waves in America. "Gangster" was a great word of Burdeyon's. It was a new expres-

22

sion at the time, and of course he was a great one for modernity. "Gangsters! Gangsters!" he would yell, striding on to some upheaval in Dining Hall. There is a story of Swabey-Boyns' of how Burdeyon came upon him taking tomatoes from a greenhouse. "Arrest this gangster!" he cried to a nearby gardener, and Swabey-Boyns was led away on the end of a rope.'

'It was Swabey-Boyns who began the chain that Burdeyon protested against. Not the Boer War one. Boyns' idea was that the letter had been started by an Indian called Mazumda. There was some fearful concoction about a god that this man was in communication with, who had the power to inflict typhoid fever if Mr Mazumda did not meet with cooperation. Boyns boasted he made seven pounds ten. Mostly from new boys.'

'Boyns was as cunning as a bird.'

'The Devil,' said Mr Sole, 'incarnate.'

They clipped the coupons out of the advertisements in two newspapers, and filled them in and prepared their envelopes. The weight of their mail was important to them.

'Hullo, hullo,' said Major Torrill, and the music began on the wireless, and Mr Sole and Mr Cridley rose to go, as they did every day, as they had done for two and a half years.

Mrs Jaraby took small rock cakes from the oven, knocked them from tins on to a wire tray and pierced one with a needle. The needle showed traces of a yellow slime, which would set, Mrs Jaraby hoped, as the cakes cooled, but which indicated nevertheless that the mixture had not been fully cooked. Her husband had told her at lunchtime of his invitation to his friends. She had reacted sharply, not because she disliked the two men – old Sole and old Cridley – but because her husband had failed, again, to warn her sufficiently in advance. He did not realize that one cannot with confidence present guests with rock cakes that have been hastily made and are still clammy within. She opened the window and placed the cakes on the sill. The sunshine caught them. Swearing to herself, she picked them one by one from the wire tray and placed them together on a plate. She put the plate in the refrigerator.

A woman preparing for a birth could not have been more pre-occupied than Mrs Jaraby. Given to similes and symbols and telling analogies, she would have accepted with enthusiasm this very comparison. For she saw the return of Basil as something that was much akin to the arrival in the house of a new child. 'If you wish for proof of my labour,' she might well have said to her husband, 'there is my single-handed piercing of your groundless opposition.' She had done more than dust and clean the prepared room. In a drawer of the dressing-table she had placed a dozen linen handkerchiefs with the letter B exotically in blue at one corner of each. She had bought a small alarm clock and she wound it every day, so that the room had a lived-in feel about it. She was determined about Basil; it might be her last battle, but she intended to win it. Basil should live in the house, and when they died the house should be entirely his. Sheets for his bed were warming in the airing cupboard.

For Mr Cridley and Mr Sole it was a journey by bus to Crimea Road. They posted their letters on the way and discussed the lunch they had recently eaten.

'The jaws of an Alsatian dog could not have managed mine,' said Mr Cridley.

'I noticed Major Torrill left all the pudding. We shall have to fill up on Jaraby's cake.'

'The last time it was some seed thing he had bought. I do not come all this way to be offered seed-cake. Should I get some biscuits and produce them if the fare is not up to much? It might suggest more care in future.'

'Biscuits would be taken amiss. It would be like taking clothes for them to change into in case we did not like what they wore.'

'Nonsense, it is not at all like that. No one brings clothes out to tea. Biscuits seem like a contribution.'

'They might take it as a reflection on their hospitality.'

'That is what it is. It is not our fault that their hospitality leaves something to be desired.'

'They do not get on well together.'

Mr Cridley clapped his hands together in exasperation. 'What has that to do with it? It does not give the excuse to starve their friends. They are as bad as Miss Burdock.'

'It will soon be time for Miss Burdock's summer outing.'

'We are talking about the Jarabys. What has Miss Burdock's summer outing to do with them? Unless you are suggesting that it is them she visits. I think that is unlikely, you know.'

'I was changing the subject. I imagined we had worn this one thin.'

'You had reduced this one to fantasy, if that is what you mean – with your talk of clothing the Jarabys.'

'I have always thought them an ill-suited pair. There is constant strain in that house.'

'I had not noticed it, though I grant you Jaraby is a short-tempered fellow. He will make a good President, I think. He is quite alive and gets things done.'

'He was a good Head Boy. That House was decadent when he took it over.'

They dismounted from the bus and walked in the sunshine through the suburban roads. They progressed as slowly as they could, having time to spare.

Voices in the hall denoted the arrival of the visitors. Mrs Jaraby wore a hat when there were visitors. She ran to her room to fetch it.

'This bloody disinfectant,' Mr Jaraby said. 'I must apologize. My wife, you know.' On account of the cat, Mrs Jaraby sprayed the house with an air-freshener. It was her habit to do so, several times a day, in the hot weather.

'I thought we might take to the garden,' Mr Jaraby went on, leading his guests through the french windows of the sitting-room. 'It is a pity to be indoors on a day like this.'

The sky was a pale, misty blue, unbroken by clouds. The little patch of grass that was Mr Jaraby's lawn was shorn close, a faded green, brown in places. Herbaceous flowers neatly displayed behind metal edging, were limp in the heat. 'Everything is dying,' said Mr Jaraby. 'I cannot carry enough water to them.'

'You need help. One cannot entirely cope with a garden, however minute. It becomes a bore.'

'Mr Sole, Mr Cridley.' Mrs Jaraby smiled and held out her long fingers. The men rose and in turn grasped them. Mr Cridley, given to old-fashioned gestures, would have liked to carry them to his lips, but feared the liberty might be misunderstood.

'Are you well, Mrs Jaraby?'

'As well as age allows me. I find the heat a penance.'

They settled themselves in deck-chairs and sat for a moment in silence.

'We are having trouble at the Rimini,' said Mr Cridley. 'The food is really quite inedible, and the smell of meat is always in the house. It seems Miss Burdock is losing her sense of values.'

'Here it is the smell of living meat: our giant cat. His food-stuffs, rotting fish, are more than nature is made to bear.' Mrs Jaraby stared in front of her, avoiding her husband's glance.

'One's nose is acute as the years pile up. Although I recall a resident at the Rimini who had lost entirely her sense of smell.' Recognizing that the air was charged, Mr Sole tried, not too obviously, to change the subject. 'A Lady Bracken. She came from Horsham. Now that I bring her to mind I believe she was older than we. So perhaps it is that this acuteness is temporary, and particular to the seventies.'

'We have a cat she does not care for,' said Mr Jaraby. 'I bear that cross, and must protect the beast from sly tormenting. You would not envy my lot in this house if you knew the details.'

'No cats, or pets of any kind, are allowed at the Rimini.' It seemed to Mr Cridley that their friend would soon suggest moving to the Rimini, since all was not well with his life as it was. Miss Burdock was adamant about animals: if he owed her even perfunctory loyalty he must make it crystal-clear.

'Miss Edge had a spotted terrier when she came. She carried it in her luggage and hoped to secrete it in her room. They say it savaged an Irish maid and was at once put down. Miss Edge had named it Bounce and may still be heard calling the word through the passages.'

Mrs Jaraby fetched the tea, and passing it round said: 'There is celebration here these days. Basil Jaraby is shortly to return.'

'That is good news,' said Mr Sole, wondering if indeed it were.

'Yes, it is a good thing. He will bring youth to the house and keep us on our toes.'

'One must keep in tune with the times –'

'We have been out of touch with Basil for some years. An awkward state of affairs. Absurd as well.'

Mr Jaraby shifted in his chair and grunted, spilling crumbs over his clothes.

Mrs Jaraby continued: 'It is only right that the past should be forgotten and the prodigal receive a welcome. It is the human thing.' She guessed her husband would not speak his mind before the guests. He feared her careless tongue in public; he had chid her often on that score, and given her thus an instrument she had not known about. 'As the future narrows one turns too much to the past. One sees it out of proportion, as though it matters.' Her scrawny hands waved about in the air, in theatrical gestures, making her point. Mr Jaraby sat with his back half turned to her. He could not see her movement, but he felt it and disliked it. 'Do you dwell much in the past, Mr Sole, Mr Cridley? Your school-fellow, my husband, does: he rarely leaves it.'

'I think we are concerned with what goes on, the world, its state and what we may expect. We tend to live from day to day, reading the newspapers and observing our fellows. We are not always pleased in either activity I may tell you.' Mr Cridley spoke; Mr Sole lent emphasis by nodding.

'Soon she will get morbid,' Mr Jaraby put in. 'Soon she will speak of death, for she believes its fingers touch us since we are old. Well, may we talk now of pleasanter things?'

Mr Sole had struck some hardness in the centre of his rock cake. He picked it from his mouth and felt it cold between his fingers. It seemed to Mr Sole to be a piece of metal, like the prong of a fork; though curious, he passed no comment on it.

Mr Jaraby began to speak of the business on the Old Boys' agenda and of plans he was keen to implement.

Often Mr Jaraby had brought home from an afternoon meeting of the whole Association a youth of eighteen years or so. Mrs Jaraby would prepare tea for both, probably running down to the shops for a jam-roll to eke out what she already had. The two men would talk together for several hours, and Mr Jaraby might well invite the lad to supper. Indeed, it occasionally occurred to Mrs Jaraby that these conversations had a quality of endlessness about them and that the young man seemed set to spend a day or two in her husband's company. Concerned almost entirely with change, the two spoke of the difference between the days of Mr Jaraby and the days, spent in the same environment, of the youth. 'Polson here,' Mr Jaraby said once, indicating his visitor, 'slept in my old bed at Dowse's. You know the bed: I pointed it out to you the last time we visited the place. Polson, do they still flick pats of butter on to the ceiling of Dining Hall?' Anecdotes, memories, the high-lights of sixty years ago: they bubbled out of her husband, and checking the changes was his happiest game. 'I recall once, Polson, I hopped the length of that Upper Dorm three hundred and forty-six times. By the time the marathon ended half the House had collected by the door. Dowse threw a sixpence on the floor. D'you know, we won the tug of war five times running?' Polson, or whoever the youth happened to be, would smile; and Mrs Jaraby, the facts engraved upon her brain, would nod from habit.

The old men talked, until by chance a silence fell amongst them. Then Mr Sole, aware of his duties as a guest, addressed his hostess.

'We got on to chain letters this morning, Mrs Jaraby. Have you ever come across that kind of thing?'

'Chain letters? The expression rings a bell. Now I cannot quite recall what it means.'

'Her mind is slipping,' suggested Mr Jaraby. 'They are letters which form a chain, foolish lady. The chain is scattered all over the world.'

'My mind is as sharp as a razor. I remember chain letters now. Basil had one during an Easter holidays. I remember copying the letter out.'

'One sent them to far-off destinations,' said Mr Sole. 'California and Italy. I seem to think the Italians were inveterate writers of such mail.'

'Basil's had to do with a certain Major Dunkers, a fallen warrior of the Boer War.'

'Good heavens, that is the same man! Major Dunkers who started the ball rolling from the battlefield. I was telling you, Cridley. What an amazing thing!'

'Were you involved with the Major, Mr Sole?'

'I was part of the chain. I helped to keep it going, and passed it down the years, it now appears, to your son.'

'I did not know they had so long a life.'

'Nor I. Think of the half-crowns that must have changed hands!'

'It must have thrived for thirty years at least. Had it become well rooted in that school that both of you were part of it? It may yet survive. Immortal Major Dunkers!'

'The Headmaster, Burdeyon, was against those letters,' Mr Cridley said. 'It surprises me to hear of a tradition like this. Subsequent headmasters could hardly have given the thing their blessing I would have thought.'

'It was a harmless pastime, Mr Cridley. I see no call for a headmaster to condemn it.'

'Burdeyon considered it as a dishonourable pursuit,' Mr Sole explained, 'with gain its only end. As I was remarking to Cridley, a mutual friend of ours, one Swabey-Boyns, made a small fortune in this manner. Burdeyon would have called that reprehensible. He was a man of violence and high principle.'

'Who, who?' asked Mr Jaraby.

'Old Burdeyon. He disliked those chain letters.'

'Quite right. A waste of time and energy. Dowse ordered me to clear the House of them.'

'Because they came from the outside world,' cried Mrs Jaraby, striking a dangerous note.

'That they did,' her husband agreed with vehemence. 'From idle pawnbrokers, Dowse said. I tore up dozens in my time.'

'Not Basil's though. I doubt if you even knew that Basil honoured the death of the good Major Dunkers.'

'Of the good *who*? What is the woman talking about?'

'He fought –' began Mr Sole.

'Do not go into it all again,' said Mr Cridley, clambering to his feet and adding: 'We thought of attending a Wednesday Compline in Putney. In which case we should be on our way.'

'It rests our minds and offsets what Miss Burdock has concocted for dinner. Though after your excellent tea we shall require very little.'

'Salami and a leaf of lettuce. It is likely to be that on a Wednesday.'

'There was part of a fork in my bun,' said Mr Sole when he had passed from his hosts' earshot.

'It might have killed you. I did not know about this Basil Jaraby. Who is he, and why did she think him interesting? I must say I had hoped for sherry. It is customary to be offered something as one leaves.'

Mr Jaraby called his wife. He cupped his hands about his lips and shouted. The cat came in from the garden and rubbed itself against his legs, clawing his trousers. Mr Jaraby went to the lavatory and shook the locked door back and forth. 'What is this nonsense about Basil? We have heard enough of it. I must forbid the name in the house; indeed in the garden too. It is outrageous that you should have spoken so before old friends. I felt my position to be intolerable.'

'It was meant to be. Please preserve the conventions. I expect peace and privacy in the lavatory.'

'Oh, rubbish. You cannot pretend that Basil is returning to the house just by stating it. You are making yourself a figure of fun.'

'I state what is to be. I do not overstep the mark.'

'Obedience is my due. I will demand it: refrain please from these references to one who is a near-criminal.'

'I speak of our son.'

'You speak of a serpent's tooth who has disgraced the name we bear.'

'He has done what you have driven him to do. You must mellow and forgive him, as he has forgiven you.'

'Has he forgiven me? For what? Did I commit some crime?'

'In terms of Basil, not one but many. Return to the garden and think. Sit in the evening sun with your cat upon your lap and reflect on your son. He is my son too, you know. Weak woman though I am, I have rights in the matter.'

'You have no rights. If you will see him, then see him. Visit the wretch, but do not impose him on me. You have no rights there.'

Mrs Jaraby had sought her present refuge for no other reason than to escape a face-to-face inquisition. She stood within the small space, sighing between sentences. 'Basil is invited to tea on Sunday, as the old men were invited today. We shall sit in the garden in the sun, as we have done in the past.'

'That I forbid.'

'Then you must forbid when the time comes. You must scuffle with your son in the hallway and prevent his entry with force.'

'You have cut across my simple desires in this matter –'

'No, no, that is not quite the story. That is not the essence of what we talk about. What we are saying is that your sting has been drawn: a part of you is dead.'

Mr Jaraby saw that his wife was mad. It saddened him for a moment that she had come so soon to this.

4

The heat continued and increased. It turned the remaining green of the lawns in Crimea Road into a uniform brown. It turned the sun-lounge at the Rimini into a hot-house. It blistered the backs of Mr Nox's hands when he sat too long on the tiny flat roof that was one of the attractions of his flat. It ripened the bulging toma-toes in General Sanctuary's glass-house and it affected Mr Turtle. It warmed his bald head as he sat through an afternoon in the park, and afterwards as his body cooled he shivered and switched on the electric fire. Sir George Ponders watched the blue stripes fade on his front door cover and mentioned the fact to his wife. Mr Swabey-Boyns pulled the blinds down, for of all things he loathed sunlight.

The eight men went their ways, living their lives as they had grown used to living them. They spoke daily of the heatwave, and to a varying degree they remembered that which gave them an interest in common.

'I shall be glad when the end of the year comes,' Sir George confessed to Lady Ponders. 'I have felt undertones of something or other at committee meetings of late. One becomes tired of sitting round a table.'

'You must not worry. You have done it for longer than the others. And being always in the Chair is now clearly a wearing business.'

'Jaraby should make a better hand of President than I did. In a way I feel I have failed in this final official position. I have filled so many, it seems a shame.'

'Mr Jaraby is still full of beans. But he is the kind of man who suddenly snaps in half, like a brittle twig, and then that is that. My dear, you have aged in a more dignified way. Gradual processes are the happier too.'

'Perhaps so. Certainly Turtle snapped into dotage in an alarming manner. He is like an old, old ghost.'

'I wish Mr Jaraby would not telephone you quite so often. Is it always necessary?'

'He is selected to step into my shoes. He imagines we have much to discuss. He has an eye for detail.'

'I would not like to be married to him.'

'No. And you are safe in saying it – there cannot be much chance that you will experience that now. It is Turtle I worry about. We must try and entertain him now and again.'

Mr Turtle was ashamed of himself. He was ashamed that he could make no hand of the loneliness that had crept upon him. He was ashamed that he could let his mind wander so, and watch it wander and not care; that he had to ask so often for words to be repeated to him, and had invented a story that he was deaf. When the committee had last met, for instance, it had seemed to Mr Turtle that the men around the table were not at all what they were but Ponders major, Sole, Cridley, Jaraby, Swabey-Boyns, Nox, Sanctuary: the boys they had been, sitting thus to arrange a rugger team or talk some inter-House business. To Mr Turtle they seemed fresh-faced and young, starting out on a life that he had finished with; patiently and kindly waiting for him to find his way from the basement to the room, and not blaming him at all, because they accepted that he should make mistakes.

'I beg your pardon?' said the man on the seat in the park. Mr Turtle repeated his question.

'Oh, it is ten to four,' said the man, and smiled. Mr Turtle nodded and smiled back. He let a minute or two go by, then he said:

'What weather!'

The man shook his head, as if to say: 'It is too much of a good thing.' It was a large head, its face pink and fleshy, with a small black moustache, and spectacles to which had been added clip-on lenses of shaded glass.

'I read somewhere,' said Mr Turtle, poking at the gravel with his stick, 'that our unreliable weather is due to bombs.'

'Ah yes, yes.'

'The flat I live in is not designed for this kind of carry-on. It messes up the food, and the woman who does for me complains. I dare say you have similar problems, sir?'

'Ah yes. I keep birds. Though originally tropical, they have by now had to become used to the vagaries of these isles. Budgerigars.'

'Little coloured ones? I have seen them about. In the houses of friends. Cage-birds they're called.' It occurred to Mr Turtle that he had forgotten to take his pill after breakfast. He rooted in his waistcoat pocket and finally brought one to light. Fumbling and unsteady, his hands were inefficient. The bones beneath the flesh seemed fragile, as delicate as chalk. 'My medicine. I cannot offer you a share. Unless you have a heart condition.'

The man shook his head. Mr Turtle said:

'Birds are interesting.'

'Ah yes.' The man's voice was pitched high, not unlike a bird's itself.

'I found them interesting as a child. Their eggs especially. I remember the thrush's was nice. Is that the greeny one, speckled?'

'My interest is in the one breed only.'

'I think it is a speckled one; unless there has since been a change. You will understand, sir, a considerable period has elapsed.'

The man nodded. After a silence he volunteered, rather unexpectedly, that the day was his birthday. 'I am forty today. Though still young, it is a blow to leave the thirties behind. This is the middle of middle age.'

'Well, congratulations.'

Abruptly the man spoke with great speed, stumbling over the

words: 'I say, look, I recognize your tie. We attended the same school. Forgive my mentioning it, but I am embarrassed about funds. Now say so at once if I should leave the subject, but could I perhaps prevail upon you – five pounds or less would see me through. I am owed a lot for birds. But you know, I sell a lot to ladies in distressed circumstances. They do not always pay on the nail.'

'Oh dear, have I misled you? I do not think I could have a bird. The woman who does for me is strict, she would not take to the trouble of an animal about the place. Mrs Strap. She is rather hard to get along with.'

'Sorry. I meant a loan. I am being hasty, I know, but since we come from the same school – well, it's a bond – though I have known you but a matter of minutes – five pounds or less would fit the bill – I could pay you back by post or in this park. I would not ask – I can promise you my credit is good – oh, shall I go? Have I embarrassed you?'

'No, sir, I enjoy a bit of company. The error is mine, I had imagined you were selling me a bird in a cage. I knew I could not manage it, and found myself in an awkwardness. I wished to refuse as politely as I could. Is five pounds sufficient? It will not go far, you know.'

'Well, seven goes further.'

'Take seven. That is my school tie I am wearing. Mind you, not the one I wore at school, but the tie of our Association. The Old Boys' Society, of which I am a committee member.'

'What I am saying is that I, too, was at the School, though in fact I do not belong to the Association. Three guineas a year is a little beyond the means of a bird-fancier.'

Mr Turtle, having parted with seven pounds and absorbed the facts the man proclaimed, became excited: an acquaintance had become a friend, or, if that was rushing things, there was at least the promise of a future for this chance meeting. He tapped the head of his stick with his left hand, flapping the fingers rapidly. He proffered his right hand for the man to shake, which the other, as pleased as Mr Turtle, promptly did.

'What a happy coincidence!' exclaimed Mr Turtle. 'You must have been there – when?'

'Nineteen thirty-seven to forty-two.'

'Well, well. I of course was much earlier. Nineteen-o-six to nineteen-eleven. Burdeyon was Headmaster. And the great H. L. Dowse died in my day.'

'Were you in Dowse's?'

'No, I was with the less illustrious – heavens, I've forgotten the man's name!'

'I was in Dowse's. I didn't much care for those years. I don't remember much about them even. Not wishing to, I put them from my mind. There was a big brown photograph of Dowse somewhere.'

'Many of my companions fell in the war. Sanctuary, who was my junior, rose to great heights. He is now a – a general. General Sanctuary, you may have heard of him?'

'Ah yes.'

'He too is – is a member of the committee. Was the food always cold at weekends? I remember that well, winter and summer.'

'Maybe it was. Your memory is better than mine. I seem to see brown, flat sausage rolls on Sundays for tea. I sat next to a radiator in Dining Hall and would put my porridge behind it. I remember that because they beat me for doing it. When they beat me I was sick. I used to vomit in the lavatory.'

'My name is James Turtle.'

'Mine is Basil Jaraby. I must go, I fear. I have seed to buy. Due to your kindness my birds shall dine well tonight. If I might have your address I will put the money in the post when, as it were, my ship comes home.'

The man went. Mr Turtle watched the baggy figure move through the quiet park and felt sorry that the occasion had not lasted longer. He should have suggested a cup of tea near by, or issued an invitation for the young man to visit him. He had been preoccupied trying to bring to mind his Housemaster's name and had allowed the chance to slip. At least he had been firm about the bird, for, though the man was kindly, a bird in a cage would have meant that Mrs Strap would be nasty. He would be obliged to show her his will again, to confirm afresh that he was leaving her a thousand pounds.

5

Mr Nox was hunched and rounded, wizened like a nut. He suffered from rheumatism in the winter, but during these hot summer months he had come into his own and felt he had the advantage of his fellows: he scarcely noticed the heat. Only when the blisters rose on the backs of his hands would he glance above him to confirm that the trouble came from a sun that was too naked in the sky. His small flat was neat and clean, every book in its place, every pencil sharpened for use. He did the work himself, made his bed, carried laundry to the launderette, sewed on his buttons, cooked his food, and twice a week ran a vacuum-cleaner over his carpets. He had been productive all his life, and had won, he felt, his way in the world. He intended to go on that way, to make no changes except the ones that were forced upon him, to earn money, though it was not much, until his brain stopped, bogged in senility. Mr Nox took pupils. He taught them mathematics or, if they preferred, Italian. He did not visit; his pupils came to him. He was urged to take more by the agency that sent them, but he wished only to work in the mornings: he knew it was easy to become fatigued and he wished to spare his strength, to spread it over several years rather than wear it away all at once. He had never taught until he reached retirement, but he found that he was good at it and he made his charges high. His pupils themselves said he was good; good as a tutor but a little dry as a man. They thought him humourless, for he did not often smile; and when he had taught them what they wished to know they tended to forget that he had played a part in their lives.

Mr Nox's bell rang. He greeted the man who stood at the door with the suggestion that they should spend the hour in the sun on the roof. The man, whose name was Swingler, seemed a little doubtful. He considered that the roof, cased as it was in lead, would be, at midday, somewhere to avoid. 'As you wish,' murmured Mr Nox, wiping the cream from the backs of his hands with a handkerchief. 'I had prepared myself for the roof, but no matter. Sit down and tell me what, if anything, you have to tell.'

'This time again there is nothing, I am afraid. I have drawn a series of blanks. You must take my word for it that I have worked carefully on your behalf.'

'Indeed. I have no option but to take your word.'

A month ago the agency had sent along Swingler. He wished, he said, to learn Italian because he felt Italian would help him in his business.

'I know little of Italian business expressions,' Mr Nox had said, 'having never had to use them.'

'I am not in that kind of business.' Swingler scratched the palm of his left hand with the fingernails of the right, making a noise as he did so. 'I am a private investigator. I run a small detective agency. Specializing in divorce really.'

Mr Nox had given him his first Italian lesson without thinking further about his pupil's profession. But the second time he came he questioned him more closely.

'You say divorce, Mr Swingler. But you take on other cases, I presume? What kind of investigating do you do beyond divorce?'

Again there was the scratching of the left palm and a twitching began in Swingler's face, for he was a nervous man.

'Very little, Mr Nox, beyond divorce. Marital troubles are, as you might say, my bread and butter. Mainly I watch people. A husband for a wife, a wife for a husband. I follow the party here and there, check on liaisons, observe, report. We do get the occasional case of someone who is dodgy in the business world, embezzling and that. And once in a while there is a wretched creature who is being blackmailed. Cases, you know, where discretion is necessary, which the police could not be trusted in. Our telegraphic address is Discretion, London.'

'Would you watch a man for me?'

Swingler was surprised. Anything was business if it was honest, he said. He laughed nervously.

'I will make a deal with you, Mr Swingler. I will teach you Italian in return for your professional services. How does that strike you? All fees, except your expenses, to be foregone on either side. Does the proposition interest you?'

'All propositions interest me, Mr Nox, you know.' He laughed again, as though apologizing for himself.

'Good. Then here are the details. There is a man who in the interests of a small proportion of the public must be promptly discredited. I need not dot all the i's. He seeks a position for which he is unworthy, let us say that and no more. I have reason to believe that there are things in his life which do not bear scrutiny. It may well be that to you the habit I am about to describe is a common one and widely practised, but to the others in this affair it is enough to make them think again. Would you like to make a note, Mr Swingler? The man's name is Jaraby, he lives at 10 Crimea Road, sw17. Mr Jaraby is in the running for the presidency of a certain society, an association of Old Boys of a certain school. Now a position like that calls for impeccable respectability, as the position of headmaster does, or that of a judge. You understand me, Mr Swingler?'

Swingler nodded sagely, agreeing, and intimating that he understood.

'This man Jaraby is an old man, older than I am. Say about seventy-two or three. He sees me, rightly, as an enemy and, wishing to ingratiate himself with me, he some months ago offered to do me a favour. Not to put too fine a point on it, he offered to introduce me to a brothel. He claimed it was a good, clean place and went into some details about the nature of the services offered. I declined, but found the information interesting. You may say that Jaraby, having made this offer to me, had given me all I needed. But you do not know Jaraby: he is a wily bird, and it is my word against his. We are all elderly men, Mr Swingler; we see in each other the possibility of poor memory and misunderstood words. Jaraby would talk himself out of my accusation as it now stands. What I need is proof, what I need is your report, signed and sealed and irrefutable. I need it in writing from a disinterested person that Mr Jaraby's practice is to visit a house of ill-fame.' Mr Nox had half hoped that Swingler would say that that was easily achieved; that all he had to do, if Mr Nox remembered the name and address of the place, was to sit down and cook the evidence. But Swingler was cagey; Swingler had a lot to lose. He said instead:

'So you want me to watch Mr Jaraby and – excuse me, Mr Nox – catch him in the act?'

'To see him enter the place once or twice would be quite sufficient.'

'You will get no statements from the inmates. They will not give away their clients, or indeed themselves.'

'That is not necessary. Just your statement on paper in combination with my reported conversation will damn him.'

'It is a difficult job. I might watch the house for weeks before he made a visit.'

'Ah, Mr Swingler, that is surely your problem.'

'It might be simpler for me to approach matters from the other end, to strike up a friendship with one of the girls and get her to tip me off when he was due to arrive – assuming of course that he makes an appointment. It would have to be cunningly done and very *sub rosa*, if you know what I mean. Like I say, they will not split on their clients, but if I handle with care we might get round that one.'

'Jaraby pressed the address on me. I can let you have that.'

'A help, Mr Nox, a help.'

But as events turned out it was little help at all. The girl with whom Swingler struck up a friendship revealed that clients came and went and no one was the wiser. One might serve a man for twenty years and yet not know his name. And there was no appointments system.

'So there is still nothing to report?' Mr Nox said on this particular occasion. 'You are keeping an eye on him, though?'

'The trouble is, Mr Nox, I cannot cast a wide net. I do not have the personnel to watch the house and our party's movements constantly. I have chosen certain times and devoted an hour or so to surveillance. He shops himself for vegetables, that I can tell you, but alas, little else.'

'The vegetables do not interest me at all. It is clear he slips away while you are elsewhere. Now, have you any suggestions?'

'Sooner or later I should catch him. We call it making a strike. Or what I may do is leave him for a while and then devote a week or more to the business. Except that we do not know how frequently he visits. The law of averages is only half on our side.'

'Time is running out. I may have to give you more lessons in Italian and ask you to intensify the operation.'

'I would watch the house you say he goes to rather than his own, except that he may have changed it or likes variety. I think a lot about the case. I feel that light will break sooner or later.'

'Sooner, Mr Swingler, rather than later. As I say, time is running out.'

'Or I may have an idea. It may be that we are approaching this from altogether the wrong angle. How would it be if we tempted him?'

'Tempted him?'

'With a woman of the kind he fancies. A casual meeting in a café or something.'

'You know best. We may have to resort to that, but I do not greatly care for the sound of it. It is his own rope with which Jaraby should hang himself.'

'Any port in a storm, Mr Nox.'

'I need evidence. I will leave it to you to sort out how you come by it. After all, it is your job.' But Swingler, who was getting on well with his Italian, was in no hurry.

When his pupil had gone Mr Nox cooked chops for his lunch. He did not like Swingler. He had got into the habit of washing his hands when Swingler left the flat. He did not like him because he could not explain to him. Swingler would not understand if he said: 'It is simply that I bear a grudge against Jaraby. He is well fitted for the task before him and should acquit himself nicely. To be wholly truthful, I am doing the Association a disservice by attempting to bring all this to light. There are skeletons in all our cupboards, Jaraby's is no worse than any other.' He could not admit to Swingler that he cared little himself for the Association, that if a less able man than Jaraby were chosen it would not matter to him as long as Jaraby was shamed in the process. Some devil within him had urged him to get himself on to the committee, so that he might, by some chance that had not then been apparent, cook Jaraby's goose. Jaraby was an influence in his life, but he could only confess it to himself. Jaraby was a ghost he had grown sick and tired of, which he could lay only by triumphing in some pettiness.

Unlike the other man, Mr Nox was not lonely. He was alone in the world and would die unmourned, but he had faced loneliness as a boy and come to terms with it then. It was like getting over measles, knowing that they had taken their toll but would not return. As he walked about his flat, seeing to his needs, he felt that he had never been young; that his life had been a mere preparation for the state he now found himself in, that this was his realm and was no imposition. As with the heat of the present months, he had the advantage over those who had grown old with him; they at an ebb, he at a flow. When he sighted himself in a mirror he knew that this was as he was meant to be, not the cranky child or the man of middle age. And often when Mr Nox reflected on these things he concluded that in his time of power he should crow over Jaraby, as Jaraby in his power had crowed over him. There was a logic and a justice in nature; he could not see that nature might be otherwise. It was not even so much the long memory of the ill Jaraby had done him that caused Jaraby to linger in his mind; it was the redress of a balance that had slumped so far out of true as to offend the senses. To tidy a human situation, that was all Mr Nox desired.

He shredded cabbage and timed its cooking. As he stood by the stove his one nagging regret slipped irritatingly into his thoughts. His life had been ordinary. He would have liked to have written his memoirs, but he knew there was nothing to write. 'The tragedy,' he sighed, 'of those who come into their own too late.'

6

'Pleased to meet you, gentlemen,' said the man in the bowler hat. He stood in the sun-lounge of the Rimini, hovering, though not uncertainly. He smiled with gaiety at the seated men. Mr Cridley began the process of identification.

'I am Mr Cridley, this is my friend Mr Sole. I cannot speak for my friend, but in my case your presence here is somewhat puzzling. We have not met; your face is new to me. How can we help you?'

'Not you me, but I you,' the man said smartly. 'My card, sir. Joseph Harp, heat exchange expert and installation engineer. I come about central heating. You have been in communication with my firm.'

'Yes –'

'I have come, in a word, to measure up and deliver you with an estimate. A biggish job, a biggish house. A good day's work, I hazard. Now tell me, sir, what did you have in mind?'

'Pray sit down,' replied Mr Cridley, 'and take off your hat.'

'You are wise,' said the man, obeying these injunctions, 'to take advantage of our summer terms. Ten per cent off. Naturally enough, a lot of people don't think of central heating in the middle of a summer like this. Well anyway, a lot of people who are not as far-sighted as you, sir. Pardon me: I've taken a liberty.'

'Not at all, not at all.'

'I spoke rather personally. I estimated character rather than what I am here to estimate. I have that way with me, gentlemen, and I hope you'll forgive. My tongue runs away on me, as any of my mates will tell you. Colleagues I should have said; we are told to say colleagues. Again the victim of my tongue. Gentlemen, you'll pardon me?'

'Yes, yes –'

'We are given a short course in salesmanship, every one of us when we join the firm. Say this, say that, never say the other. They tell us how to lead a prospect on, watch for the nibble and time the moment for the kill. It's very exciting.'

'What's a prospect?' Mr Sole asked, genuinely interested.

The man aimed a wild blow at his thigh, punishing himself for his shortcomings.

'Forgive me, forgive me,' he cried. 'Aren't I running on like a dose –? Oh my God, you'll think me a frightful fellow! A prospect is a person, gentlemen. A person you aim to sell something to. A prospect is a customer before, if you follow me, he becomes a customer. A prospect is a prospect is a prospect. That's a little joke we have in the trade. A kind of a jingle that we call out to each other when we meet.'

'What does it mean?' asked Mr Sole.

'What does it mean? Well – gentlemen, do you know, I don't know. D'you know, I've been saying that for a fair number of years now and –'

'We are mightily intrigued by all this,' Mr Cridley interrupted. 'I think I speak for my friend as well. We are interested ourselves in the world of business, of salesmanship and advertising. We are not professionals, you realize, but we watch and learn. Your advent is little short of a tonic. That is not flattery, Mr Harp. Mr Sole will tell you fast enough I am not given to flattery. No, I feel we could talk together all day –'

'In the way of central heating, Mr Cridley, just what did you have in mind? We have the Major Plan, the Minor Plan and our –'

'We are interested, Mr Harp. We are very interested indeed. But my friend and I are of a conservative nature. We do not care to rush things. I call upon you, Mr Sole. Is that not so?'

'We do not care to rush things, no. It is true we are interested, and we would greatly like to know about your system. We would esteem it a personal favour.'

'No favour at all, gentlemen,' Mr Harp retaliated briskly. 'It is why I am here. Part of the day's work, part of the job, part of the service. For a house the size of this I would not hesitate to suggest our Major Plan. Warmth, warmth, and more warmth, eh? That's the ticket in a place like this unless I'm much mistaken. I note you're in the hotel business. I put it to you, gentlemen, that a snug room is heart's delight for the weary wayfarer. Am I right, gentlemen, or am I wrong?'

'Without a shadow of a doubt –'

'I can mention no prices until I've seen the premises. A thorough inspection. Nooks, crannies and how's your father? Right, gentlemen? The cellars are my immediate interest. It is usual to begin in the cellars, to establish the siting of the boiler. Once the siting of the boiler is out of the way, Robert becomes your avuncular relative. Ha, ha, ha,' laughed Mr Harp briskly, drawing papers from a briefcase. 'Lead me to the cellars.'

Mr Cridley and Mr Sole rose slowly, eyeing one another. They followed Mr Harp who had, so he said, a nose for the geography of a house.

In the cellars Mr Cridley coughed and said:

'You are moving rather fast for us, Mr Harp. Strictly speaking, a lady called Miss Burdock is in charge here. We are at a disadvantage. Mr Sole and I would wish to talk the matter over –'

'Mr Cridley,' called Miss Burdock from the top of the stairs. 'Mr Cridley, what are you doing down there?'

Mr Harp, quick to assess a situation, replied: 'Miss Burdock. Is that Miss Burdock?' and began to mount the stairs.

'I am Miss Burdock. Mr Cridley, who is this man?'

'Joseph Harp, madam, and here with a purpose. Heat exchange expert and installation engineer. Central heating is my stock in trade. You want it, Harp has it. OK, Miss Burdock?'

'I do not want central heating, Mr Harp.'

'This is the Rimini Hotel? The gentleman below, Mr Cridley? I have you on my list.'

'Be gone, Mr Harp.'

'Now wait one little minute, madam. Now –'

'Be gone, please. Promptly and without further argument vacate the space you stand in.'

'Madam –'

'I shall not hesitate to complain to your employers.' She held the door and Mr Harp passed through. 'Mr Cridley and Mr Sole, do not skulk in the darkness. You must face me and explain all this.'

'My beautiful Boadicea,' murmured Mr Sole, stumbling behind his companion up the cellar steps.

General Sanctuary pulled the straw hat over his eyes and fell asleep. He dreamed that he was talking to the Prime Minister on the telephone. 'There is one man in the country,' the Prime Minister was saying, 'who has the know-how and military skill to salvage what is left of this unholy mess. You, General. I know I do not ask you this in vain. Let me hear you say you are ready, General.' The garden was peaceful in the warm afternoon. Bees and insects droned lazily amongst the flowers. Strawberries ripened. Pods of peas were full and yellow; asparagus shot into seed, its fern delicate against the untidy earth.

The General had been re-reading Henty, the only author he cared for. *For the Temple* lay open beside his chair, its leaves curling as he slept. He had read the book a dozen times or more. He could quote long passages from all the works of G. A. Henty, and quite often he did.

'There is only one man I can call upon. You, General Sanctuary.' The dream was not entirely a fantasy. Once upon a time, many years before, a Prime Minister had addressed him in terms that were not all that dissimilar.

Basil Jaraby set about his weekly task of cleaning the cages of his budgerigars. He slid out the trays and cleaned them one by one. He scrubbed the perches with a wire brush and washed out the water- and seed-cups. He examined with care the toys they played with – pieces of furniture designed for dolls' houses, bells and little wooden trucks – satisfying himself that they had not become damaged and might be a danger. The birds seemed in good spirit, although he spoke to them anxiously, worried in case the heat was affecting them harshly. The room was not ideal for their habitation: there was a danger of draughts if he opened the window, and if he kept it constantly closed he feared for their welfare in an airless atmosphere. He prepared their evening meal of seed and a little grass, put fresh cuttlebone and millet in the cages. He taught the cleverest one how to walk up and down a miniature step-ladder, and began his taming of another, offering it his finger as a perch.

Mr Swabey-Boyns was engaged on a large jigsaw of the Houses of Parliament. It was very difficult and he wondered if he would live to finish it. A month ago, in hospital, he had completed a smaller but no less difficult one of Ann Hathaway's cottage, and had then upset the whole thing over the bedclothes. The nurses had laughed; and he had laughed later, as he clipped little holes in their sheets with his nail-scissors.

Mr Turtle broke his rule and thought about his wife. She had died during the First World War, when he was in France, after they had spent only two days together. She caught pneumonia, and in the bustle and confusion of wartime no one had been able to tell him how it had all happened or how she had died. Films, to which Mr Turtle was addicted, made such stories romantic, but to him the reality was scarcely sad even: it was ugly and precise and a fact.

Once Mr Turtle had kept photographs of his wife, faded sepia prints that became absurd as the years advanced. There was nothing of her in them, just a face that was now a stranger's face; for in his mind he had forgotten what she looked like and remembered more poignantly other things about her. He tore the photographs up, without any emotion at all. But often, and more often recently, he found himself weeping. He did not know why until, in a cinema or on the street – because it happened more usually when he was out – he wiped his leathery face with his handkerchief and thought the matter out. Then he knew that some passing detail had reminded him of his wife. He scolded himself and said he was behaving like a child; weeping in the street like that, causing people to pity him, inviting them to approach him and enquire about his welfare. So he made up the rule, promising himself to be on guard against the memory of her.

But Mr Turtle had just been to see a re-issue of *Random Harvest*. It brought back the war to him, the ins and outs of emotional entanglements and the setting off by train for the front. He had seen it through twice and had watched the opening scenes once again. He emerged with a headache, feeling shaky in the legs and syrupy all over. Over a cup of tea in the cinema restaurant he tried to straighten himself out. He took a pill, ate two pieces of bread, and tried to convince himself that he was feeling quite gay: he drummed his fingers on the table-cloth, humming a tune. He would telephone Cridley and Sole and see if he might visit them at the Rimini. The journey would waste an hour or so and they were always quite refreshing, the things they said. He remembered Cridley using a terrible obscenity once in the washroom, and that little fat clergyman who was the Housemaster overheard him and thrashed him, as he stood there in his pelt, with everyone watching. The little fat clergyman was always thrashing people when they did or said something wrong in the washroom. Years later there had been some scandal when a couple of Old Boys returned and thrashed the little fat clergyman.

Mr Turtle made his way out of the restaurant. A waitress ran after him to explain that he hadn't paid for his tea. He gave her the money and went on his way to telephone the Rimini.

'It is scarcely a month,' complained Miss Burdock, 'since those frightful women came here with corsets. And now a man with central heating. You can guess what I am going to say to you, both of you: if there is further trouble I shall be obliged to ask you to leave the Rimini.'

'A genuine misunderstanding, Miss Burdock, a genuine error.'

'I could easily fill your rooms. There is a waiting list for the Rimini.'

'Now now, let us not be hasty.'

'Let you not be hasty, Mr Cridley. Nor you, Mr Sole. You escape with a warning, but make no mistake –' The words hung ominously in the air. Miss Burdock, like a monument driven by some propulsion outside its nature, sailed from the sun-lounge. Mr Sole and Mr Cridley returned to their newspapers.

'Free trial,' said Mr Sole. 'Send no money. Retain for ten days, return if not delighted.'

'What is it?'

'Transistor Company of Great Britain. A wireless set.'

'You know, I have it in my mind to get in touch with Harp. We might arrange to meet him outside somewhere and have a drink. I was keenly interested in what he had to say for himself –'

'Take care, take care. We must not offend the threatening manageress.'

'We must not nothing. We are free, white and over twenty-one. Burdock has gone hysterical.'

'I know, I know. But she can soon have us out on the street.'

'Nonsense. If we meet Harp in the quiet seclusion of some bar, what harm is there in that? If we meet him as a friend what can Burdock do?'

'Still, care should guide us.'

'So it shall be. I shall telephone Harp and arrange a conference. I'll tell you what,' Mr Cridley added, leaning forward and lowering his voice, 'it's this hot weather that's affecting Burdock. You understand how disastrous a run of heat can be for the ageing virgin?'

7

The cat Monmouth, feathers adhering to its jaws, strode possessively through the french windows and sought what it might destroy. Its single eye gleamed voraciously, passed from carpet to cushions, over stacked-up magazines and Mrs Jaraby's knitting basket, stared at its own reflection on the empty television screen, lighted on the smooth fabric of the curtains and stretched out an exploratory claw. The curtains slid away beneath the pressure and the cat humped its back. In anger the claws stabbed at the carpet, and Monmouth, baring a massive jaw, snarled at the tufts of wool.

'Oh puss, puss,' cried Mr Jaraby, 'what disorder is this?' He smote the cat heavily on the rump, for although he was fond of it and enjoyed its company, his sense of discipline did not permit this ravaging of his property. Monmouth leapt across the room, spitting and screeching. 'No, my puss, it will not do. We must mend our ways. We must bend to the greater authority.' Mr Jaraby dropped to his knees and effected a perfunctory repair on the carpet, stuffing the strands of wool into his pocket since he did not wish to dispose of them immediately. He sat at his bureau, and Monmouth in a faithful way lay beneath his chair. As was his wont, Mr Jaraby spoke to himself.

'She takes no care to purchase goods at the right time and in the right condition. I have myself to see to the vegetables and fruit. She will not stand up to the shop people and say: "Split the produce in half that I may see inside." How else to know if an apple or a grapefruit is worth its money? I get the better of the shop people; why cannot she? It is all embarrassing. She will not see a doctor. A doctor would give her tablets. She should have sedatives day and night; no one can come to the house without noticing that something is amiss. This wild talk. No one could stand this talk. Did Cridley and Sole not note it and shake their heads? Do they not perhaps discuss it and pity me in my distress? They will say it, all of them soon: "Jaraby's wife knows sanity no more." They may condemn me even for not having her seen to or taken away, yet my hands are tied; I can do nothing, since she will recognize no shortcomings in herself. There was madness in that family, her mother had staring eyes, her father drank. There was a lad at school hanged himself from a tree. I never knew till Dowse revealed the truth and put me on my oath to hold it to myself. They gave it out he had fallen from the branch, these things are better under cover. Dowse was the wisest man I ever knew. I tell you, she brings groceries to the house that I have forbidden here. And now she calls for her son.'

'She calls and he shall come,' said Mrs Jaraby, entering the room. 'He comes to tea on Sunday.'

'So you have told me. Not once but many times. You must be humoured. I will receive my son in kindness to you only. My feelings remain. You know the truth and cannot face it.'

'I know the truth and do not have to face it. I faced it in the past. I accept the consequences of your actions. Have I an option?'

'You are wandering in your mind.'

'My mind is a sounder possession than it has ever been. I think clearly and I know what is to be.'

'You sit before the television with the sound turned off. Tell me now that that is not a nonsense. Is that a healthy mind in a healthy body?'

'Oh, these awful tags you use! What is the meaning of that phrase and how can it apply to me? My mind has survived my body. I am grateful for that if for nothing else.'

'You have a roof above your head to be grateful for. You have every comfort in this house. What pleasure can you get from voiceless faces on a screen?'

'You do not hear the sound because your ears are less sharp than mine. I do not like everything at an unnatural pitch.'

'A doctor would set you right. A doctor would give you tablets to clear your confusion.'

'You are a hypochondriac on my behalf.'

'I have the evidence of my eyes and ears.'

'Unreliable organs, dimmed by time. Beware of what a doctor might say of you.'

'You are being malicious because my thrust has struck home. I have all my faculties about me. How else do I hold my position on the committee, in busy communication with thousands?'

'Your trouble is the faculties themselves, not the loss of them. Your cat has damaged the carpet. Soon there will be nothing left of this house. He has eaten wallpaper and may yet attack us as we sleep.'

'Monmouth is an old and gentle thing, seeing out his days. He would not harm a living thing.'

'He harms the birds, he is feared by local dogs. Have a stout cage constructed that he may see out his days in some less gruesome way.'

'You pick on an innocent cat! Your cold nature cannot endure a pet that might be a comfort to me.'

'My cold nature cannot endure a pet that may slay us in our beds.'

'That is wild talk again. Have you heard of such a thing, a cat responsible for such an act? How can you speak so irrelevantly?'

'Monmouth is the kind to set a precedent. It would be a rich end for us both, we would feature in Sunday papers!'

'Leave death alone. You talk of death and dying all day long. Can you not imagine what it's like to hear a woman speak of death from morning till night? Have you no perception?'

'I spoke lightly. But your cat eyes me jealously. He would like the flesh off my bones! My jest may yet reverse itself on me.'

'I have simple ways. I cannot continue with this kind of thing. I came here to read through Basil's school reports and such letters as there were at the time.'

'Basil is grown by now. It is not yesterday. Basil is forty.'

'I am aware of it. Who more than I should know that Basil has lived that long? The forty years have not been free from trouble, you know.'

'Why bring up school reports? What significance have they now?'

'They lead us into his character and may be a subject for conversation when we face the awkward occasion.'

'You have not seen your son for fifteen years and you propose a discussion of his school reports! Who is being irrelevant now?'

'I regret that I mentioned this. My perusal of the reports is merely to refresh my memory. Cannot you see that I am doing my best to meet you half-way over this? I want to think the whole thing out in retrospect; to view our son's life and crimes and see how the picture looks proportionately thus. Do you not follow my simple reasoning?'

'You could ask me, I would tell you. It does not take school reports and thinking out to find the truth.'

'Why should I ask you? Since in this, as in most matters, your opinion is unreliable. Why should I waste my time, listening to you and picking out once in a mile of talk what is of the least value? I prefer to go on my own way.'

'To start with the schooldays and not the reports might get you somewhere. But in fact you must cover previous ground, before the schooldays. Come to those days in their time, assess their damage fairly. View the case-history objectively, not as a father.'

'You offer advice where none is asked. How can I examine the facts except as a father? Since I am the father.'

'Then take responsibility as a father. Do not play hide-and-seek with the issues. Basil should never have gone to that school.'

'I did not hear you right.'

'You did. But I can easily repeat what I said.'

'Why should he not? Let us have what is at the back of this. What harm did the School do him? Remember I went there too.'

'I am unlikely to forget that. Put your question another way: what good did it do him?'

'It made – it opened the world for him.'

'It made a man of him? You do not think so. It opened the world for him is devoid of meaning.'

'The School showed him the way. He could have moved in any direction.'

'You are adopting an odd turn of phrase. What you say is a string of clichés.'

'You blame the School? You blame his alma mater for subsequent sins? Be careful, woman, you will say more than you can justify.'

'In which case you will win the argument, and then at least one person in this room will be satisfied. Like your cat, who sleeps well-gorged beneath you.'

'You are away from the point. Stick to what we are discussing. Or is Monmouth, too, an implement in Basil's downfall?'

'What an absurd suggestion! How could a cat have anything to do with this? That school was not wholly to blame. Say it finished what already had been well begun.'

'I will not say that. I do not understand it. My School was good enough for me, why not for Basil? He did not shine there, I grant you that. He rose to no great heights, he won no prizes. Was that the School's fault?'

'He was afraid of the place. It was you who rose to great heights and won the prizes. He was to do likewise. He tried, God knows, but a frightened child can achieve little.'

'Woman's talk! You have the unhealthy relationship that women have too often with their sons.'

'We do our best. We are made as mothers. We cannot help ourselves.'

'Why should the boy have been frightened? What was there to frighten him? I was not frightened; why should he have been?'

'He was another person, brought up in other circumstances.

Your own ghost was at that school. And you were here at home. What chance had he to escape?'

'You are attempting to undermine me, to bring me low. There are veiled insults in every word you speak. You have nothing to say and you make up nonsense as you go along. You should see a doctor. When Basil comes I shall bring this up. He will be sorry to see you in this state. The School is five hundred years old; its sons have distinguished every walk of life. Yet irresponsibly you refer to it as though it were some worthless, crackpot place. I would remind you that I am shortly to become President of the Old Boys' Association of the very school you malign. Such disloyalty is obnoxious; and, if I knew the law, might well give me a case for having you put away. I ask for silence.'

'Ask for it you may, but have it you shall not. There is a threat in what you say. It is a rubbishy threat and I choose to ignore it. Do not lock yourself within yourself. See yourself from beyond, as other people see you. Change shoes with them occasionally. You shall have your silence now. You need not worry about what I say. I have been speaking academically: it is too late to speak in any other way.'

The silence fell, and it was Mr Jaraby who broke it. In his reading he had come upon passages he could not help quoting.

'Biology. *A studious pupil, thoughtful and interested*. Well, that is something; that shows promise, I think. And this in the same report: *Geography. Maps, excellent*. A good term for Master Basil. Alas, all of a sudden we have dropped off. *French. Idle and lackadaisical. He makes no effort. Algebra. He shows no evidence that he has grasped even the elements of this subject*. Very uneven, up and down like a jack-in-the-box. Here's Latin Composition the following term: *First-class work. He has applied himself assiduously all term. History*. Quite good. Not a dunce, you know. By no means. Are you listening?'

'Yes, I am listening.'

'*Dear Mr Jaraby, Basil's Housemaster has had occasion to inform me* that your son's present attitude is causing him some little concern. Your son persists in a disobedience which, while concerned with a mere detail of school routine, is nevertheless a disobedience. He has been punished no less than eight times on this count, sometimes quite strictly. I have caned him myself and spoken severely to the boy, but I now learn that the trouble still persists. I would ask you, Mr Jaraby, to speak to your son about this matter during the holidays. I need hardly say it would go against the grain to have to ask for the removal of the son of an Old Boy, but I trust and am confident that it will not come to that. Yours sincerely, J. A. Furneaux. P.S. The trouble has something to do with pouring plates of porridge behind the radiators in Dining Hall. I remember that. My God, I remember that letter. I never felt so ashamed in my life.'

Mr Jaraby continued to look through his papers, dozed for a while and awoke with a sniff.

'She ruined the boy. She should see a doctor and have done with it. She's a damned nuisance.' He spoke to himself, although his wife was still in the room.

8

Basil came to tea at Crimea Road, but the occasion was not a successful one. Basil was silent, listening to his parents in turn, agreeing by gesture, nodding and smiling a bit. His eyes seemed drowsy, reflected twice in the thick lenses of his spectacles. He is taking drugs now, thought Mr Jaraby; and bit back the inclination to accuse his son thus. Mrs Jaraby was worried mainly by the condition of Basil's clothes. He wore a striped suit with a waistcoat, of a heavy cloth that made no concession to the weather. Here and there it was burnt and marked, and seemed generally to be dirty. Dandruff clung to its collar and lapels, bird-seed in small patches to waistcoat and trousers. As well, Basil wore boots. They were army boots of rudimentary design, black and unpolished, surplus stock he had bought for a pound. 'Do you eat enough?' Mrs Jaraby asked, offering him rock cakes. There was an unhealthiness about his plump face, and she remembered his lung trouble as a child. How could this man be the baby she had nursed? How could the crinkled body have grown so swiftly to this? Had he, she wondered, been real as a child, learning to speak, teething and falling over, or was he real now, middle-aged and shuffling before his time? The line that connected the two images faded and was gone: for all she knew, the man who ate her rock cakes might be an impostor. 'Your mother is addled in her mind,' Mr Jaraby said when she had left the room. 'I urge her to seek the attention of an expert but . . .' He made a hopeless gesture with his arms. Basil seemed to be thinking of something else.

Mr Jaraby had referred to the school reports and had spoken at length of the Old Boys' committee. During all this his wife had shifted impatiently, sighing and uttering short cries. She attempted, while her husband spoke, to engage Basil in a separate conversation.

'Are you happy?' Mrs Jaraby asked as he left, when her husband had already made his farewells and was watering plants in the garden. 'Are you happy where you live and in what you do?'

'Happy?' He spoke as though he questioned the meaning of the word, as though he might draw a dictionary from his pocket to check or confirm its connotation.

'Are you happy, Basil, in your life now? Would you care to live with us here? Would that be easier for you?'

'I have my birds. I am happy looking after them.'

'You would not have to cook or make your bed. You would not have to clean and dust. Your old room is as you left it. Sheets and blankets in the airing cupboard.'

'It is kind of you.'

'You would find it less expensive, your food and lodging no longer a draw on your purse.'

'I could not.' Having said it, Basil sought round for a reason.

'Oh come, it is not like you to be proud. It is your due. We are your parents. He owns the house and it shall pass to you when we die.'

'I could not bring the birds here.'

'Why not? We can take to the birds as well as other people. We would soon grow used to their chirping.'

'It is not so simple.'

'I have had to accept a cat that is little short of a monster. What are a few birds in comparison?'

'It is the cat I fear. Cats and birds do not see eye to eye.'

'You are afraid Monmouth would injure your budgerigars, is that it? Monmouth is old, he has not long to live. Without a cat about the place you would think differently?'

'Oh yes. My birds are quite valuable. After all, they are my livelihood. I cannot take risks.'

Basil left, and Mr Jaraby, his watering completed, returned to the sitting-room. 'So that is our son,' he exclaimed, easing himself into an armchair. She did not reply. She felt in no mood for conversation.

'Come, puss,' Mr Jaraby said. 'I shall talk to you. What did you think of our Basil? Ah, old Monmouth, you are the only comfort this old man has left. We age together, my cat and I. Are we not two of a kind? Plagued and tormented by the cold nature of a woman. Ah, you are purring. You do not purr often, my cat, and I not at all. How good it is that you are happy on your master's knee at the end of this trying afternoon. Your master is almost happy too, for he has one loyal friend –'

'Such slop!' cried Mrs Jaraby. The simplest thing, she reflected, would be to do away with the cat. Although it would have suited her better to do away with them both.

Basil, his head aching, walked slowly from the bus-stop to his room. The outing had rather tired him. 'You remember that letter, boy?' his father had said jovially. 'The porridge behind the radiators? How important it all seemed then! How serious and black-browed we were! You scarcely spoke all holidays. I remember being quite stern.' Basil remembered other things: putting his father's bicycle-clips down the lavatory, giving his father's ties to a tramp, collecting slugs, putting earth beneath the cushions of an armchair, smoking paper and trying to smoke coal in an old pipe. One of the first things Basil could remember was eating a rasher of bacon, raw. He remembered the feeling that led to it: the instinct that it was something he should not do, and was not meant to do, although no one had actually forbidden it. He hid it in his pillow-slip and ate it when the lights were put out. He persevered, although the taste was nasty; he wept over it, his stomach turned and heaved, and as he swallowed the rind he was sick all over the bedclothes. At school Basil had done these private things too: he had taken five shillings out of Martindale's jacket pocket; he had torn all the centre pages out of Treece's *Durell and Fawdry*; once while ill in the sanatorium he had left his bed late at night and watched one of the maids undressing through a chink in the curtains; he had followed Rodd major and Turnbill with binoculars.

Such memories, begun by his father's reminiscing, streamed through Basil's aching head as he covered the ground to his room and his birds. He wished he had not gone to tea: this upset to his routine was something he could not take in his stride. His mind would play on it, and these images from the past would annoy him far into the night. They were all too close to the surface, too easily accessible to be taken risks with. He should have foreseen it, he should have remembered his father's penchant for the past and guessed that by going to the house at all he was playing with fire. He sighed, giving seed to his birds and cleaning their trays to occupy himself. He wished there was somewhere to go or someone else who might talk to him. He cooked a tin of beans and wrote briefly to A. J. Hohenberg.

Dear Mr Hohenberg, Thank you for yours of Monday. All goes well with me and mine, although I am a trifle concerned about the chick I bought in Norwich in January. He has grown fast and has a good voice but still seems cramped in movement. He is beginning to moult and appears feverish – could this be psittacosis? Do you know the symptoms? If it is, can you suggest a treatment? Naturally, after the experience I had with Rubie some months ago, I do not wish to embark on anything drastic, but would be grateful for a certain and safe cure. My hopes that the little one might turn out to be pink have been brutally dashed. He has grown as blue as the sky and I shall dispose of him soon, for I feel one should not have to live with a broken promise. Sincerely yours, B. Jaraby. P.S. I hope all is well with you.

Later that evening Mr and Mrs Jaraby spoke again.

'It is not that I cannot hear the sound,' he said. 'There is no sound to hear the way you have regulated the set. You sit there knitting and watching the actors mouth without speech.'

'It is more amusing. One can study the acting and make the most of faces.'

'My God!'

They had married when they were quite young. Then she had

been more humble, coming from a family in which humility in children and honour shown to parents were golden rules. It was only quite recently that the humility had worn away; only recently that she had ceased to please and ceased to make allowances. She went her own way now, angering him as frequently as she could: by purchasing Australian food, which he forbade in the house because he had a prejudice against that country; by refusing to cooperate in the matter of the fruit and vegetables; by failing to place water on the table at mealtimes, although she had unconsciously done so all their married life; by stirring up trouble with Basil where none need be; by inviting him to tea and threatening that he should again live in the house; by mocking his cat and his affection for it.

Mr Jaraby did not wish to devote this large proportion of his time to a consideration of his wife. He had his work on the committee to do, letters to write, ideas to develop. Even now he should be lobbying his fellow committee members to ensure, to make absolutely certain, that the way was clear for his presidency. He should be thinking about Nox and judging what it was that Nox had in his mind and how, when the time came, Nox would jump. Yet his wife's attitude sapped his time – having her always about him was like being ill. He would have to do his lobbying at the School on Old Boys' Day. He would speak to them one by one, extracting where possible a definite promise of support. 'Ground has been lost,' he said to himself, but when he mulled over the situation a little longer he reckoned he would easily recover it. He turned a knob on the television set. Dialect voices filled the room.

9

'Pardon me, sir,' cried the woman, jostling Mr Jaraby at the counter in Woolworth's. 'Have I damaged you? I was rudely pushed.'

'No damage done. There is a rough crowd here on Saturdays.' He proceeded on his way, but the woman pursued him, brushing his jacket and holding on to his arm. 'One longs for more elegant times,' she cried, smiling at him, not anxious to let him go. 'Do you live in these parts?'

Mr Jaraby, startled by the woman's directness, replied that he did. She fell into step with him. 'It is a pleasant neighbourhood, though not at all what it used to be. You have seen changes? Have you lived here always?'

'Well, yes, I have –'

'How nice to get to know a neighbourhood so well! How nice to feel a native!'

When Mr Jaraby entered the greengrocer's he found the woman still at his side. He spoke to her of the vegetables and made recommendations, assuming she was there to buy. But when his order was completed, when the assistant turned to her, she said: 'No, no. I am with this gentleman.'

'I have forgotten your name. Forgive me. Have we met before?'

'We met just now in Woolworth's. Shall we meet again?'

Mr Jaraby, finding the woman a nuisance, raised his hat and crossed the street, leaving her safely trapped by traffic on the other pavement. But when he sat down for a cup of tea in the Cadena she was there again, begging permission to share his table. 'Meringues!' the woman cried. 'Shall we gorge ourselves on meringues today?'

'I have already ordered a bun. But by all means take meringues yourself.'

'I must watch my figure, but having met you I shall go on the spree with meringues. You are not overweight. Well-built but without surplus.'

Mr Jaraby did not speak. The woman continued:

'I have trouble with liver. It leads to plumpness. I have injections for it.'

Mr Jaraby did not reply. He felt embarrassed, sitting in a café with a stranger who spoke about her liver. The waitress brought his tea and he lengthened the process of pouring it and buttering his bun. He had no newspaper to read. He tried to look over the woman's shoulder.

'Meringues,' she said to the waitress. 'I am having a fling! The heat,' she continued across the table – 'isn't it terrible? It is no weather for a plump girl, I can tell you. I sleep quite naked, with only a sheet these nights and the window thrown up.'

'It is oppressive, certainly.'

'I can see you are a gentleman. Do you mind my saying it? I love a gentleman. My secret is I fancy men who are no longer young. Wise with years, but young in their ways. I think I see you are young in your ways.'

'I am seventy-two. My age shows and often I feel it. My wife is a year older and quite out of control.'

'Ah, I do not care for wives! I am naughty about that. Tell me now, is your wife as plump as I am?'

'Well, no. My wife is like a skeleton. A bag of bones.'

'Perhaps you prefer the skinnier woman, eh? Am I not your sort? I can make arrangements –'

'Excuse me, please. I would prefer not to talk like this.'

'You are shy, dear man! Come on now, if you would like me to make arrangements –'

'Arrangements? Arrangements? Madam, you have the advantage of me. I am at a loss –'

'I have friends who are attractively thin. No tummy at all. Upright like sticks, no –'

'Are you confusing me with someone else? I cannot continue this conversation.'

'Or younger ones. Thin or fat. One of them trained for the trapeze. Another a mass of muscle, she used to be a gym teacher. Bus conductresses in uniform. Canadians and Chinese. Girls in kilts or macintosh coats. Lady disciplinarians. Girls come back from the Israeli Army. Blacks and old grannies. Ex-nuns. Judo girls. Greeks.'

She was as crazy as his wife. The world was full of wretched women. Did his wife, he wondered, behave like this, talking madly to strangers when his back was turned?

'Shall we meet again?' the woman cried, but he was moving fast to the pay-desk. She shrugged her shoulders and pulled a face at Swingler, who was sitting a table or two away.

Outside, Mr Jaraby noticed a young constable on the beat and considered for a moment reporting the matter to him. He decided against it, for it would take so long to explain; the policeman would be stupid; he would be asked to go to the police station; he would be asked if he wished to bring charges. Mr Jaraby knew this, because often before he had made complaints to the police, though never a complaint as bizarre as this one. He found the police obstructive and politely impertinent. He had once had cause to take part in a long correspondence with a Chief Constable concerning the impudence of a desk-sergeant. He did not wish to go through all that again. Yet he was conscious of a mounting anger against the woman. That broad, hideous face, coloured like a parrot, ill-fitting teeth dangling in its mouth, the whiff of perspiration, the awful, endless chatter of nonsense. Dowse had given him, man to man, the address of a safe house which boasted an exclusively public school clientele. Dowse had told him about disease, about young men fresh at the University getting themselves into a mess. He had quoted histories, spoken of the terror in a young man's mind that led so often to total decadence or suicide. Dowse it was who had given him, though on another occasion, the address of a good tailor and had recommended a barber's shop in Jermyn Street. Dowse would have made a man of Basil, no doubt of it. It was odd how these things were: how influenced and – yes, the word was right – how inspired one might be at a certain age. The formative years. Dowse stood no nonsense. *Fight fairly, squarely, have nothing to hide, indulge in no shame*: the words might aptly have been inscribed on his gravestone. And with the thought of his gravestone he remembered the roar of the hymn in Chapel that had marked his passing, and the silence that followed it. With Dowse as his master, Basil today would not be training a circus of birds in a hovel of a house somewhere. There would not be this estrangement in the family, with Basil a bone of contention between man and wife. Well, estrangement there was and so it should remain. Polite Sunday teas were one thing; Basil beneath his feet all day, birds fluttering through the house – that was another matter, and one which he did not intend to tolerate. How dare she think along such lines! What was there to be gained, from anyone's point of view, by a son returning at this late stage to live like a child with his parents? Did she wish to wash his hair and bathe him, to buy him Meccano sets, to send him spruced and combed to Christmas parties?

How few people there were in the world, Mr Jaraby reflected, who were equipped to weather it and remain intact and sane. What pricks in the flesh one endured: one's wife, one's son, a crumpled cripple like Nox, this woman who leeched on to him. Dowse had said Nox was a trouble-maker. 'He plays no games, Jaraby. He shows no enthusiasm. The strictest surveillance for that boy, Jaraby. The task may not be to your liking, but we are all together in the House, we have a duty one to another.' He had failed with Nox; he had tried and he had failed. Nox today was scarcely a creature to be proud of. Could one say without flinching that one had been an influence in his formative years? Yet his instruction from Dowse had been that he should be. 'These are important years, Jaraby. The man is made, his standards are set.

67

See that you leave your mark on Nox, as you leave it on others. I know you well, Jaraby. I trust that mark.' Mr Jaraby laughed. One could certainly not be proud of the absurd Nox.

His steps had led him away from the shops and the crowds into a leafy suburban road not unlike his own. He entered a house that was marked with a brass plate, consulting his watch to check his punctuality.

Dr Wiley, who was elderly too, was dressed in an old-fashioned manner. The knot of his tie was noticeably large and had not been pulled into the familiar position on the collar. It left a gap of an inch or so, in which a brass stud featured prominently. In combination with his wing collar and the cut of his waistcoat the stud contrived to suggest a tail-coat, although in fact Dr Wiley was not wearing one. Mr Jaraby came straight to the point.

'She is far from herself, Doctor. She rambles in her speech and makes no sense.'

Dr Wiley played with a magnifying glass on his desk, holding it over random sections of print. He liked to have something in his hands when he was giving a consultation. He came straight to the point too.

'Is she fit physically?'

'It appears so. She seems strong as a horse. She can lift things and do a day's work.'

'Ah. She must not lift things too much. Nor do too strenuous a day's work. She is no longer young. We forget how taxed the body becomes simply by living a long time. See that she does not overwork. Get her to put her feet up.'

'That is not the trouble. She talks of having our son to live with us; she has had him to tea.'

'An extra person in the house certainly means extra work. Does she have help?'

'A woman comes. It is wild, irresponsible talk that worries me more.'

'Can you be specific? What kind of things –'

'My dear man, I'm telling you. Our son, she says, is to come to

68

live in Crimea Road. In his old room which she has prepared. He will bring his birds.'

'Now, Mr Jaraby, that does not sound wild. Your wife feels she would like to see more of her son. It is natural for loneliness to creep in at this age. Be a companion to her more, if you can. Do you ever go together to the cinema?'

'Go to –? Heavens above, what good would going to a cinema do? You cannot cure madness in a cinema.'

'But is there madness to cure? You have given me no evidence of it.'

'We had cut our son off. We had not seen him, nor cared to see him for fifteen years. Well, I think she occasionally called on him – but at least he never came to the house. He was not welcome, he was not invited.'

'And Mrs Jaraby thinks of a reconciliation. That is very natural. It is quite normal and in order –'

'My son, Dr Wiley, is a near-criminal. He has been in trouble. We do not discuss it. Basil is a great disappointment to us.'

'To you. Maybe not to your wife.'

'Oh, rubbish. You know nothing of it. You are speaking outside your province.'

'I am attempting to help you. You came for advice.'

'That is not true. I came for pills or tablets to calm my wife. You are deliberately obtuse.'

'Come, come, Mr Jaraby, let us keep our tempers.'

'Let us keep to our proper places and not overstep the line. I repeat, Dr Wiley, Basil is a near-criminal.'

'Be that as it may, I cannot prescribe for your wife –'

'Oh my God! Great God in heaven, why cannot this said case –'

'If you shout, Mr Jaraby, I shall ask you to leave.'

'I am not shouting. You are not listening to me. Are you refusing to treat my wife?'

'Certainly not. Mrs Jaraby is my patient. I will call and talk to her, examine her if necessary.'

'What good will that do? This is really too much. I have had a trying day. My wife goes on. People annoy me on the street. Yesterday there was the strain of Basil in the house again. I make a simple request; a good doctor would instantly accede to it. It is useless to talk to her. She will consent to nothing.'

'If you consider that I am a bad doctor you are at liberty to have another. I remain your wife's, though. Is it your wish that I visit her?'

'No, it is certainly not my wish. I never suggested it. When did I ask you to visit her? What are you talking about?'

'Then that is the end of the matter. Unless you can persuade her to come to me.'

'Is that likely? Give me pills or tablets that I may put in her food.'

'My dear Mr Jaraby, I cannot do that.' The Doctor laughed to ease the atmosphere. 'I would be struck off the register.'

'You will see this woman suffer? You will see me suffer? She would take no pills herself. The mad think the world is mad. You should know that. After this I cannot believe you are a fully qualified doctor.'

'I must ask you to go.'

'I am going. I shall seek medical aid elsewhere. You are a callous man, far beyond the work you try to do. My fingers itch to write the facts to the Medical Council.'

'I can give you the address.'

'You are cheap and insolent, incompetent and doddering. Your brass plate shall be in a dustbin before the month is out.'

With his stick he struck the brass plate fiercely as he passed it, scarring his knuckles and noticing briefly in its gleam his blood-red, maddened face.

If I will it well enough it shall come to pass, she thought. He shall come with his birds in cages and release them through the house at the times he wishes. They shall chirrup and chatter and I shall watch him teaching them to say a few words. The past shall stay where it is, forgotten and never again raked over. He shall eat good meals, stews and tinned fruit, biscuits with his coffee. I shall wake in the mornings and hear the sound of the birds, and take an interest in them and go with him to shows. People shall come to the house to see them and buy them, not people who are old and lonely and of uncertain temper, but men who talk enthusiastically of their interest, who can tell the quality of a bird and can talk about it, so that one may learn in time to tell it too, and exchange a point of view.

10

On the day that Basil went to tea in Crimea Road, Mr Turtle went to tea at the Rimini. He was quite a regular Sunday visitor and had come to know many of the guests besides his two friends. With Miss Burdock he was a favourite, who saw in him – at least by Mr Cridley's theory – a potential source of exploitation as a possible resident at the hotel. On this particular occasion Mr Turtle found his friends absent.

'Where they have got to I cannot imagine,' Miss Burdock said. 'They do not often go out on a Sunday afternoon.'

'I telephoned. I wouldn't come unexpectedly.'

'Forgetful old men! No worry, Mr Turtle. We shall enjoy ourselves.'

'Oh yes, we shall. I just wonder what has happened to them. They wouldn't have met with some accident? You'd have heard?'

'Now no worry, please, Mr Turtle. We shall enjoy ourselves. Your friends are off on a raz-dazzle.'

They sat together in Miss Burdock's cubby-hole off the hall. She was repairing a sheet, stitching it by hand. Bills and receipts were neatly arranged on long upright spikes on her desk. Beside them, a first-aid box and a pair of rolled-up stockings.

'I have just again seen *Random Harvest*,' Mr Turtle volunteered. 'A great work. Have you seen it, Miss Burdock?'

'Many years since. I found it very, very touching. Fancy your going to the cinema.' She wore pince-nez for sewing. On her large face they seemed like an ornament, tiny and nearly lost.

'I often go. I am quite a fan.'

'And I, Mr Turtle. I go to the Gaumont on Tuesdays.'

Mr Turtle thought. He felt his mind slipping away, sliding from the moment and the conversation. He pulled himself together, fearing his silence would offend.

'On Tuesdays? Would we perhaps join forces one day? It is nice to go with a companion.'

Miss Burdock beamed, her hands suddenly still, her head thrown to one side. 'Well, that would be pleasant. On a Tuesday some time?'

'Certainly on a Tuesday, if Tuesday is your day.'

'Tuesday suits me perfectly. It is not always easy to get away from the hotel. So much to see to. Supervision is unending.'

Mr Turtle sighed agreeably. 'What a worry, poor Miss Burdock!'

'Providence calls me. I love my old souls. Simple fare and a wireless, nothing more they ask for.'

'I have, you know, a whole house to myself. It is sometimes a bit much; empty rooms are depressing.'

'But, Mr Turtle, you are not married. How do you manage? Who sees to you and cleans? Don't say you equip yourself with dustpan and brush?'

'I have a Mrs Strap who comes by day, in the mornings.'

'A Mrs Strap?'

'That is her name. She is a youngish woman, very particular.'

'I know the kind. I have had them at the Rimini. Out for what they can get and don't give tuppence how they get it. What a bane she must be for you!'

'Well, she knows the work and keeps the place tidy. She cooks a lunch and prepares cold supper. I manage my breakfast myself.'

'Dear me, it does not seem at all the thing. Here at the Rimini we are all friends together. My job is to worry, my guests are free as birds. We eat like kings and rest and chat. We are the happiest family in the land; not one of us is lonely.'

'It is nice to have someone to talk to.'

'At the Rimini we talk all day. Chatter-chatter, like a cheerful band of monkeys!'

It would be nice to have a little bird in a cage. He had thought the man was trying to sell him one, a little blue budgerigar which he could teach to speak.

'On Sunday mornings,' Miss Burdock went on, 'we have a service here in the hall for those who cannot manage the walk to church. They do enjoy it. Mr Featherstone arranges the chairs, Miss Edge plays the piano. We have a prayer and a hymn and I give them a thought for the week. When old Mrs Warren died she said as she passed: "Miss Burdock dear, give me a last thought. Give me a thought to carry from you to our Father." Those lines of Bunyan sprang to mind. I took the old lady's hand in mine and said: "My dear, you have lived by hearsay and faith, but now you go where you shall live by sight." Ere I had finished she had given up the ghost.'

'The lady died?'

'At rest and happy. Glad that the end had come in her beloved Rimini.'

You had to slit their tongues to make them speak, but all that would be done by the man. While she was in the house he could keep the bird-cage in his wardrobe, and she need never know.

'You've come a Sunday too soon,' cried Mr Cridley in the hall. 'We expected you next week, old man.'

'My friends are back.'

'The reprobates return!' she carolled merrily. 'Safe and sound and exercised. Scold them, Mr Turtle, while I prepare your tea.'

In the sun-lounge Mr Sole and Mr Cridley told about the visit of Mr Harp, and were cantankerous about the part played by Miss Burdock.

'Perhaps I should live here,' Mr Turtle said. 'You have a bit of fun.'

'Don't be rash, Turtle. This is a frightful hole. Miss Edge crazy on the upper corridor and Torrill taken away now because he cannot control his natural functions. You wouldn't find life in the raw as spectacular as you think.'

'I like Miss Burdock. She always has a word for me.'

They had attempted to get in touch again with Mr Harp.

Mr Cridley had telephoned a number they discovered in another advertisement for the same central heating. He tried twice and Mr Sole tried twice, but each time they were told that Mr Harp was out on his rounds. They were nervous of leaving a message, in case Mr Harp telephoned them at the hotel and Miss Burdock was rude to him again.

'You would have liked him, Turtle. Interesting about a world we are quite unfamiliar with. What they teach these salesmen to say, how they lead a prospect on.'

'I know. Salesmen come into films. They cannot pronounce certain words. A lot of them are American.'

'Don't speak of this in front of Burdock. She is silly about people like that.'

Miss Burdock, majestically bearing a tray of tea and sandwiches, entered and set to dispensing its contents.

'Mr Turtle dear, have they apologized?'

The men were at sixes and sevens, groping their way to their feet to herald her entry, seating themselves to receive her bounty.

'The error has been cleared. In fact it was mine, it seems.'

They ate and drank, the two residents displaying obvious displeasure at Miss Burdock's decision to join them. They growled, murmuring through crumbs of bread with tuna fish on it. When she retired their irritation remained, turned against one another.

'We went to the Jarabys' last week. It was Sole's idea to bring them clothes as though they were refugees. I could not make him see that one does not do such a thing; but I refused to visit a draper's.'

'Did you, Sole? Did you buy clothes at a draper's?'

'I think he did,' said Mr Cridley. 'When my back was turned I imagine he obtained the clouts he hankered after.'

'You know I didn't. You are making a story of it. I drew an analogy. It was you who wanted to bring them food.'

'Food is a natural thing. A gift one carries, like chocolates to a theatre or fruit to an invalid.'

'We were not going to a theatre.'

'I am using the example to explain. You will say next the Jara-bys are not invalids.'

'Nor are they.'

'Quite, quite.'

The conversation petered out. When it was renewed the subject was the coming Old Boys' Day at the School, and with the change the discord slipped away.

'Shall we three travel together?' Mr Sole suggested.

'You mean – you mean I should join you?' Mr Turtle was pleased. 'How very generous, Sole.'

'By all means,' urged Mr Cridley. 'Sole can be generous when he makes the effort. I'll tell you what, we are thinking of taking a cruise to Yalta. Show Turtle the cruise literature.'

Mr Sole found coloured brochures in the magazine rack, handed them round and read aloud from one of them: '*It is not easy to resist the allurement of those brilliant coral reefs, those blue lagoons, those blessed palm-green shores*. Mind you, that is not Yalta. Cridley is more set on Yalta than I am. I favour the allurement of the Caribbean.'

'As far as I can see,' said Mr Cridley, 'you can have eight cabins for a hundred and eighty-seven pounds. *There is a well-equipped laundry where passengers' soiled linen can be laundered at reasonable cost*. That is a useful thing . . . *All pets should be placed in the care of the ship's butcher*. Is that a little odd?'

'Does it go on to explain? I would not care to hand my pets to a butcher.'

'It says that a governess is in attendance, but does not touch on the fate of the pets. It says that passengers must be in possession of a valid International Certificate against smallpox.'

'*Buoyant island with a happy heart. Craftsmen create tasteful pottery and play a mean game of cricket*. That is Barbados. Now why do they say a mean game of cricket? That is an unpleasant and gratuitous remark.'

'. . . *On board will be found Ladies' and Gentlemen's Hairdressing Saloons . . . an orchestra is carried . . . children are cared for . . .*'

76

'This one offers Christmas in sunshine and balmy beaches of southern shores . . .'

'You are turning my head,' cried Mr Turtle. He examined a picture of southern shores. Then he added: 'Your Miss Burdock has consented to accompany me to the pictures. Isn't that kind?'

'She is not our Miss Burdock,' Mr Sole giggled, winking clumsily at Mr Cridley. 'By the sound of it, old man, she is fast becoming yours.'

'You are welcome,' said Mr Cridley. 'She is a thorn in the flesh here.'

'I was married once,' Mr Turtle murmured; and, forgetting that he had told them before, he told them again.

When he had gone they nodded knowingly. 'He is trying to get that wife out of his system.'

'There was a time,' Mr Cridley claimed, 'when his ploy was to propose to the woman who cleans for him. He is starting work on Burdock, poor old devil.'

'Heavens above! Burdock will gobble him up. Often she has asked about his money. She is a ruthless bitch.'

'Is this true? It is poor news, Sole. Turtle would be better dead.'

'She is a lot younger than he. She sees him passing on and will collect a fat cheque.'

'Tell the spider woman to hold off. He is our friend after all.'

'Tell her? Tell the wall!'

'Dinner, dinner, you two,' cried Miss Burdock. 'The old gentleman has invited me to the pictures. Shan't I enjoy that?'

Mr Cridley was being fanciful when he said that Mr Turtle had proposed marriage to the woman who cleaned for him. It was true that he found the strain of his marriage tragedy difficult to bear and had, especially lately, regretted that a second alliance had not come about to take away the bitterness of it. But he had never seen his cleaning woman as a contender for his hand. She was a source of terror to him; the kind of woman who seems designed, certainly physically, to be a source of terror to somebody. Mrs Strap, Aries, was forty-five, small, breastless and elaborately decorated: costume jewellery, ear-rings, hair a glitter of gold. There were touches of green about the rims of her eyes, powder the colour of a burst peach on her cheeks and nose. Despite the lipstick that marked her lips far beyond their natural boundaries, her mouth remained pinched and uninviting, metallic almost, as much like the slit of a long-healed wound as H. L. Dowse's had grown to be. This comparison did not occur to Mr Turtle; he was not, in such matters, an observant man. Mrs Strap was more of a blur to him; a useful fury, an ill-tempered necessity. When she snapped, her eyes lit up with anger, matching her tongue. They blinked and glowed behind elaborate spectacles; spectacles that were a confection of bric-à-brac built up to a pair of tapering points: specks of coloured glass that were not for seeing through, with gold, or something, in triangular blobs at either hinge. That was Mrs Strap, to whom Mr Turtle had assigned a thousand pounds in his will and whom he did not wish to marry. As different from Miss Burdock as chalk from cheese.

Miss Burdock was patient with him when he was slow on his feet on the way back from the cinema. He was sleepy too, and glad of the support of her arm. They had Ovaltine together in her little cubby-hole, and when he dropped into a doze she offered him a spare bed for the night. He thanked her, explaining how much he would like to stay, but remembering that Mrs Strap would be alarmed at his absence in the morning and might telephone the police and the hospitals, her fingers crossed for his death. He did not know how he had become so tired, except that he had got himself into a state in the cinema when he found that the shoe which he had somehow kicked off was no longer at his feet. Miss Burdock ordered him a taxi, and in a clear voice gave the taxi man his address.

Swingler said: 'Maybe you're thinking you're getting a raw deal, Mr Nox?'

Mr Nox, like a neat sphinx, opened exercise books, placed pencils ready for use. He paused to ask:

'Why? We have made a bargain. Let us stick to it.'

'Mr Jaraby was unaffected in the teashop. I saw him myself. Unmoved, untempted. Embarrassment was the height of it.'

'I never liked the idea. A somewhat obvious and, if you'll forgive me, vulgar way of attaining our ends.'

'I am to continue to observe him?'

'That is the understanding.'

'The chances of success grow dimmer.'

'Where there is chance at all, pursue it. You do not know it, Mr Swingler, but already our plans are bearing fruit. I confess I had hoped for one fell swoop, a clean thrust and sudden achievement. That, it seems, is not to be. But another thing is happening. We are building up a case against Jaraby. He has spoken in a certain suggestive way to me. An unwitnessed incident, I know. But as well he has been seen by you, a disinterested observer, taking tea with a professional fallen woman. You would sign a document to that effect?'

'But the woman was in my employ. I knew what to expect, I followed the two of them from the street to the teashop.'

'My friends are not interested in you, Mr Swingler, whom you employ or whom you pursue on the streets. Why should they be? They wish to see the picture at a later stage: Jaraby and this woman ensconced together, enjoying themselves. That should be your statement; only that is necessary for the purpose.'

'This is unethical.'

'Unethical? You would be stating the truth. I do not ask you to lie. I would not do such a thing.'

'I would be lying by inference, by what I leave out.'

'Come, you are splitting hairs. I repeat, we cannot bother my friends with a lot of unnecessary detail. Like myself, they are elderly. They tire if too much is asked of them.'

'We play the Machiavelli, eh?' Swingler laughed. Mr Nox did not.

'Let us now get on with our lesson. Frankly, I dislike discussing the other matter.'

'Right you be, sir. *Uccelli o animali, fiori in colori brillianti* . . . Page fifty-seven, exercise nineteen.'

'Is that Mr Harp?'

'Harp speaking.'

'Ah, Mr Harp, Cridley here. My friend and I were wondering –'

'Whoa up a minute. I have the pleasure of addressing . . . ?'

'Cridley. Of the Rimini Hotel, Wimbledon. We met a while back. Mr Sole and I –'

'Are you the gentlemen who led me a bit of an old dance? Big rambling house, old folks, lady in long clothes?'

'That's it, Mr Harp.'

'Well, Mr Cridley, it looks to me as though our negotiations are at an end.'

'Mr Sole and I were wondering if you'd care to join us in a little drink?'

'Oh I –'

'And continue our discussion.'

'Now, Mr Cridley, I do not understand you.'

'We thought it would be nice to have a drink in some local place. Not here, you understand.'

'I'm in the dark, sir.'

'We're interested in your work and would like to know more. About what they teach you –'

'Ha, ha, ha,' laughed Mr Harp, and put the receiver down.

II

It was true what H. L. Dowse had said: a boy in his time had hanged himself from a tree. Years after the occurrence the facts had leaked out; related deliriously, it was said, by a dying master who had allowed the story of an accident to affect his conscience. By then it didn't matter. No boy of that generation remembered the incident, or had even heard of it. Five years is a generation at a school; three generations had passed.

With the truth, however, the tree became famous. New boys were led to it; it was pointed out to parents and timid sisters. Certain rites concerned the tree; certain odd little ceremonies. 'If you walk round it,' a boy once told his brother, 'if you walk round it three times slowly, it will bring you bad luck: boys have been expelled.' The younger boy, fresh from prep school and anxious to prove himself, walked as he was dared and was not expelled. But on the way back to the school buildings he tripped and broke his knee-cap. So the legend of the tree grew. It came to be said that if you smoked within sight of it you would be caught by the Headmaster himself; that if you passed within ten yards of it at night your mother would be found dead in the morning, or, if you had no mother, your closest female relative.

'Religious superstition finds a perfect example in Symonds' tree,' an atheist has recently claimed at the School Debating Society. He spoke at length about the tree, deploring its fearsome effect on naive new boys, demanding that the tangle of myths be officially denied. Christianity as a religious superstition did not enter his argument. He knew what he was about. The tree was part of the School, was closer to the root of the matter; the School was society, and he spoke in terms of what his hearers knew.

'The School may do as it likes,' H. L. Dowse had said. 'It may keep its own time. It may be almost entirely self-supporting. It may train its own small army; print and publish its own propaganda. It may invent traditions, laws and myths.' At the School a man once taught the boys in his care that New Guinea was part of Canada, that steppes were steps, that the Danube flowed through Spain. He used no text-books, and allowed only the maps he drew himself on the blackboard. They found him out eventually, but many still carry with them his strange geographical images. The School belonged to itself, adapting what it decided it required. 'A miniature of the world,' said H. L. Dowse to every new boy he interviewed. But once, later in his life, he said instead: 'The world is the School gone mad.'

The School itself was spread over a great area. Gothic blocks, quadrangles, formal gardens, statues set in cloistered niches, tablets of stone and flights of steps. Porches, pillars, Grecian urns, oaken doors with iron handles. Battlements and fire escapes, flag-poles and war memorials. Small new buildings in the old style, but those of recent years moving away from it a bit: music-rooms, classrooms, recreation rooms, laboratories, called after the men who had given them. The Headmaster, following the lead of his predecessors, said that the Chapel was the centre of school life. But his pupils would have disagreed with him, for the centre of school life varied with every boy.

On Old Boys' Day there was a cricket match between the first eleven and the Old Boys. It began in the morning and continued all through the day; but it was not, as it were, the pivot of the day, not the main attraction. The day was not like that; it was designed without a centre, without a climax; it was a centre and a climax in itself.

Cricket formed an agreeable background of hushed applause and the smack of ball from bat; white figures in distant formation, moving with dignity, small and rather strange. The cricket seemed as endless as the sea, while Old Boys, not engaged in it, stood in groups talking of past events. There were exhibitions of photography, of printing, woodwork, art, pottery, metalwork, bookbinding. The Old Boys weren't very interested: the exhibitions were really for the parents, who had visited the School on Open Day a week before.

Lady Ponders disliked the day. She quite enjoyed sitting in the sunshine watching the cricket, although she did not fully understand the game. More, however, was expected of her: as wife of the President she was obliged to sit next to the Headmaster at lunch and be led away by the Headmaster's wife afterwards, to the lavatory, which was all right, and then to the rose garden, in which she had no interest at all. She had to keep up a conversation with the Headmaster and his wife, a rubbishy conversation that flagged after every remark exchanged, and had to be tended and repaired so that a dozen times during the day it might emerge from its own ashes. Lady Ponders knew, and she knew that the Headmaster and his wife knew, that the convention was a little absurd. The Headmaster was interested in boys, she presumed, not in Old Boys; his wife, like Lady Ponders, probably in neither. Lady Ponders enquired as to the number of boys in the School. Wearily, though with a smile, the Headmaster explained to her the construction and organization of the Houses. She listened attentively, wondering about her daughter who had written to say she was seeking a divorce.

Late in the afternoon, when stumps had been drawn, there was a service in Chapel, called the Reunion Service. Old, favourite, forgotten hymns were sung and a little of the emotion that had accompanied them in the past was briefly recaptured. *Those returning make more faithful than before* . . . That hymn had little logic on Old Boys' Day, or, if it had logic, it was of a morbid order, but the hymn was always included: the most emotional of the lot, most popular of all. In the evening there was Old Boys' Dinner in Dining Hall, speeches and much hilarity. The few wives who attended the occasion had a meal with the Headmaster's wife in her private dining-room. Wives did not come in very great numbers, or very often, perhaps once in a lifetime. Lady Ponders felt it a kind of duty, not to the Association or to the School, but to her husband, who was a little lost without her. After dinner there was a second performance of the school play, the first being on Open Day. Usually it was Shakespeare or Gilbert and Sullivan. Once it had been Oscar Wilde and once, a mistake, Ibsen. This year it was *The Mikado*. Then the guests would disperse to local hotels for the night, or motor back to London.

General Sanctuary sat by himself, watching the cricket. He did not know why he came. He had begun the habit five or six years ago and had not missed an Old Boys' Day since. The school was a hundred and eight for one. The School always won. It had won when he was a boy, and it still won now. He remembered that for the School eleven the game was the dullest of the season.

'General Sanctuary, do you mind if I sit here beside you? I will not speak.'

He looked up and saw a blue linen dress and a rather pretty straw hat. The face that came between them was familiar, but only just familiar: he could not place it. The face moved. Lady Ponders said:

'We met last year. I am Lady Ponders.'

General Sanctuary smiled and rose. 'Of course sit down, Lady Ponders. Do not feel you must not speak. I am glad of a companion.'

'I escape while I may. George has disappeared. I have lunch to face and things to think of to say. The day stretches long ahead.'

'You should not bother to come. I suppose I feel it makes an outing for me, otherwise I would be contentedly at home. Each year I half look forward to it and then regret my presence. The older I become the more I feel one knows so little about oneself, one's motives, et cetera.'

Lady Ponders nodded.

'One can see others more clearly. One does not have to send another person to a psychoanalyst. One does not need to. Am I making any kind of sense?'

'I think so, yes.'

'You are being polite. The chances are I am talking nonsense. I have talked so much in my time I see no reason for a change now.'

'One collects a little wisdom.'

'Ah yes. I think that is right.'

From her husband Lady Ponders had learnt that General Sanctuary had done, and achieved, much: more than her husband, far more than the other Old Boys, more probably than anyone here today.

'You speak modestly, General.'

'Do I? It is not deliberate. It is not an affectation.'

'I did not mean that. I meant that you could afford to be conceited.'

'I wonder. It does not look like it now, as I re-enter childhood.'

'There are compensations in age. For instance, two younger people, man and woman, could not speak as we speak. I could not say to you at any other age – except a more advanced one – that you have elements to be conceited about. You may think, though, that I shouldn't anyway; that I am being a bore.'

'We are neutralized, is that what you mean? I agree, it is a good experience. Flattery between man and woman becomes simply flattery. One can speak one's mind without being misconstrued or without being doubted.'

'When the old meet as strangers, as we do, they are at their best. They may be direct and need not pretend. I must pretend with the Headmaster's wife and she with me. If she were my age the relationship would be simpler. As it is, I could so easily offend her. How I wish we could cut away all these frills!'

'The middle-aged are most susceptible, are easily hurt and most in need of reassurance. They are strait-laced in their different ways, serious and intent. They have lost what they have always been taught to value: youth and a vigour for living. They suspect their health, scared to lose it too. The prime of life is a euphemism.'

'Yet more happens in middle age –'

The General agreed. 'Everything happens in middle age. One is old and young at the same time. One bids farewell and prepares. One's children begin the command they later take over completely. It is true for instance that an old man grows to be an infant. He is regarded by a son or by a daughter as he himself once regarded them – as a nuisance, a responsibility, something weak and fragile; something that must be watched and planned for. Think of a man in middle age. He is father to children and parents both, and he must see two ways at once. One dies in middle age, certainly one is well beneath the net. We are lucky, Lady Ponders: it is pleasanter to be over seventy, as it was to be very young. Nothing new will happen to us again. To have everything to come, to have nothing to come – one can cope. Pity our middle-aged Headmaster and his greying wife.'

'But there are still little ambitions, still things one would wish to do –'

'You are right to call them little. They are slight and petty, and often unworthy of us. As the greedy ambition of the baby may be unworthy of the man he later becomes. Look, another wicket has fallen.'

'I scarcely know what wickets falling means.'

'Do not bother to discover. I could tell you all the rules and laws of cricket, but it would only be unnecessary information to carry about with you. Cumbersome and dull.'

'I would forget by next year – no, there needn't be a next year. George will not be President, I shall not feel obliged to help him out.'

'I'll say it too: I shall not come next year. When the time arrives I know I shall. I have had what people call an iron resolve all my life; to leave it behind now is rather a joy.'

'Is that another wicket fallen?'

'Three for a hundred and twenty. The Old Boys are doing better.'

There was clapping as the batsman returned to the pavilion. He walked slowly, his bat beneath his arm, peeling off his gloves, his face without expression. The sun was high in the sky, dazzling and powerful. The next batsman strode to the wicket. Three balls were bowled and allowed to go their way. One was a leg bye, another seemed almost a wide but was not given as such. The umpires lifted the bails. It was time for lunch.

Mr Nox glanced round the Dining Hall. It hadn't changed since last year; it hadn't changed very much since he was a boy. The ceiling was still stained with the marks of butter, flicked there from the points of knives. For a hundred years this habit had been maintained; today, as in the past, boys were beaten once or twice a term for indulging in it. The same House Cups stood on the same pedestals on the walls, above the antiquated radiators that Basil Jaraby had slopped his porridge behind. Had the cutlery lasted? It was thin and worn, but Mr Nox could not remember what the cutlery in the old days had been like. He remembered a boy snatching his away from him on the first day of his first term. The boy had done it nastily, keeping the cutlery until the meal was over, forcing him to eat meat and potatoes with his fingers, and to wait for someone else's spoon before he could eat his semolina.

'Hullo, Nox.'

Cridley, Sole and Turtle sat opposite him, crowded together as particular friends used to sit. For a moment he imagined they might begin some mockery of him as a twosome or threesome had often mocked someone on his own.

'Turtle is getting married,' Mr Cridley said, laughing about it. 'Turtle is a blushing bridegroom.'

Mr Nox thought it was a joke. Turtle could not seriously be getting married; Turtle had worn worse than anyone; how could he be? Who would want the old man?

'Surely not. Are they pulling your leg, Turtle?'

'Turtle is to marry our landlady,' said Mr Sole. 'The insanely beautiful Miss Burdock. A white wedding in September.'

'They are making fun of me, Nox. I am marrying again, that is all. Miss Burdock of the Rimini Hotel has consented.'

'But why?'

'Two people alone who like one another's company. Isn't it natural? People get married all the time. At a greater age too.'

'They coo like doves at the Rimini. Turtle calls for her, they go to cinematograph shows.' Mr Cridley was pointedly mischievous, employing the dated word to remind Mr Turtle of his period. The development was beyond him. He and Mr Sole had accepted their impotence in the matter, regretting it and hoping for some upset in the arrangement.

'I would not recommend this,' Mr Nox said, staring at his plate but not referring to the food. 'You are set in your ways, Turtle; you could not take a change in your stride. Any woman is an unknown commodity. Have you thought that she might bring you sorrow? You had much better see your days out on your own.'

'At least she would take Mrs Strap in hand. I cannot manage Mrs Strap on my own. And there are other reasons too.'

'You never married, Nox?' checked Mr Sole. 'I did, of course; Cridley never.'

'That does not mean,' protested Mr Cridley, attempting a leer, 'that I have not had my share of women, that I do not know about them and all their ways. I chose the shelf, I was not left there.'

'I have pupils now who are women,' Mr Nox put in, 'though frankly I prefer the company of men. Women are apt to irritate.'

'It must be fun,' said Mr Cridley, trying out his leer again, 'to have pupils who are women. You are all alone with them, are you, one at a time? Anything might happen.'

'What on earth do you mean? Are you being offensive, Cridley? Are you insinuating?'

'Nonsense, Nox. Eat up your peas. I am in a jovial mood, pulling your leg as Turtle's was pulled.'

'Women vary just as much as men.' Mr Sole, oblivious that a jarring note had just been struck, plunged into the silence it left. 'My wife was different from Miss Burdock, as different as Nox is from Cridley. Or Turtle from George Ponders.'

'They do not vary *quite* as much as men,' a younger man contributed. 'They have babies. That makes them feel a lot in common at a certain time.'

'I do not follow the logic of that,' Mr Sole said coldly. 'This was a conversation between four friends.'

'The old ones stand corrected, they know too little,' snapped Mr Cridley. 'This hearty fellow, interloper in our privacy, sets us right at once. I am reminded of the traitor Harp.'

'You none of you know anything of women,' cried Mr Turtle, a pale blush on his cheeks. 'You have no right to judge my marriage to Miss Burdock, to cast your sly aspersions. I have experienced the loyalty of one good woman, so I shall experience the loyalty of another. That is the end of the matter. Do not speak of it again today.'

There was a knocking from the Headmaster's table. Chairs scraped. Grace was said.

12

There was a new classroom block.

Mr Jaraby examined it disapprovingly. It seemed a little gim-crack to him, a little out of keeping with the main buildings, worse even than New House, that architectural monstrosity that had appalled so many in the early thirties. Mr Jaraby should have felt proud. The Association had contributed handsomely at the time, and he himself had been instrumental in the organized dunning of its members. He sought the Headmaster, not so much to register a complaint as to express a hope that the pro-jected annexe to the Chapel would not follow a similar pattern.

'Those iron window frames, Headmaster!'

The Headmaster, who detested Old Boys for a private reason, smiled.

'They displease you, Mr Jaraby?'

'Do they please you? Can they please anyone? What a cheap, nasty building after all our efforts!'

'The age we live in, Mr Jaraby, the age we live in.'

'I saw the plans, they did not look a bit like what has gone up. Were they altered?'

'It is difficult, is it not, to make much of architects' plans? They were approved by the Governors, by Lord Glegg who gave us the bulk of the money, by the Old Boys' Association and incidentally by me.'

'Let us pray the Chapel annexe will not come from the same mould.'

'That is far in the future, Mr Jaraby. What luck we have had with the weather!'

'What?'

'How goes the cricket? Shall we bend our steps in that direction?'

When he was President there would be no question of his wife attending this gathering. There was no need for Lady Ponders today. Simply, he would behave as an unmarried man. It would be like her, who had never taken an interest before, to develop suddenly an interest while she was in her present condition. As though divining his thoughts the Headmaster asked:

'Mrs Jaraby? Is she well?'

'No. She is far from well. She is in a sad, sorry state.' He would have liked to continue, to go into detail and tell about his visit to Dr Wiley. But there was no need to shout it from the roof-tops. Already it was widely enough known that he was married to a mad woman.

'I am sorry to hear that. Is it perhaps this hot spell of weather?'

'It may well be. I have heard of that kind of thing. There is no way of telling; personally I have little faith in the medicos of today. Let us talk of something pleasanter. Who is this young man who is to take over Dowse's?'

'He is a good man, I believe. Certainly he comes with a high reputation.'

'He has much to live up to. I refer to Dowse, not his successors.'

'Ah, Dowse.'

'Dowse,' said General Sanctuary who was standing near by with Mr Nox. 'We shall not forget Dowse, eh, Jaraby?'

'*I* shall not,' said Mr Jaraby, and the Headmaster slipped away.

'Dowse,' repeated General Sanctuary. 'The most sinister figure I ever encountered.'

'I was speaking of H. L. Dowse, our old Housemaster.'

'So was I. So am I. H. L. Dowse was perverted, sadistic, malicious, and dangerous. He should never have held that position.'

'But Dowse –'

'He hated all boys, possibly all people. He was a misanthrope of the deepest dye. He had so many peculiar tricks you couldn't keep count of them.'

'Really, Sanctuary, this is a lot of nonsense.'

'I well remember once he invited me to his room, opened a small notebook and read me some of the filthiest stories I have ever heard. When I made some appropriate remark he hit me thunderously across the face. I thought my nose had been broken, but I had the presence of mind to threaten to report him to the Headmaster. Whereupon he promptly desisted and begged me to spare him. He was an old man, he said, the disgrace would kill him. Imagine that to a child of fifteen!'

'Dowse was not above a bit of man-to-man smut. He saw it as part of conversation. Don't tell me you've never told a smutty story, Sanctuary?'

'Mainly at school. At school such stories were half one's education.'

'That's an exaggeration. And Dowse cannot defend himself against your slander. I never heard anyone say such a thing of him before.'

'Everyone took it as a fact. At least I've always assumed so. Surely I am right, Nox?'

'Of course, of course. Dowse was half crazy.'

'Nox's opinion –' Mr Jaraby checked himself. 'Really, I've never heard such balderdash.'

'Dowse used to tell boys they were going mad. He used actually to recommend brothels to boys who were leaving, claiming that he knew them to be free of disease when in fact he had specifically ascertained the opposite.'

'Be careful, Sanctuary. You are going too far. I cannot stand here and have Dowse maligned like this. You know I think highly of him.'

'I only speak the truth.'

'It is not the truth.'

'Everyone –'

'Everyone nothing. He was a good man, he did wonders for the House. It is Dowse's House today, after his name.'

'It is typical hypocrisy that it should be.'

'It is only fair. You have got some grudge against H. L. Dowse. So has Nox.'

'My only grudge,' replied General Sanctuary, 'is that the man half killed me.' He laughed and Mr Nox laughed with him.

'You couple of old fools, you don't know what you're talking about.' His voice had risen to a high-pitched shout. General Sanctuary spoke to calm him.

'Never mind, Jaraby, we probably don't. Dowse was a fine upstanding fellow, eh, Nox?' And the two men, who didn't much care for one another, laughed again.

But Mr Jaraby, walking alone towards the cricket field, was angry and upset. He had always thought Sanctuary a level-headed, sensible fellow. And what was he doing hobnobbing like that with Nox? Nox had a sly poisonous tongue and would make trouble where he could. Mr Jaraby, not for the first time in recent weeks, felt himself beset by idiots and sinners.

He slipped into a deck-chair. The players were coming on to the field again; the School had declared at a hundred and twenty for three, and now fielded. Nox used to keep the score at cricket matches; Mr Jaraby seemed to recall someone once telling him that Nox eventually became scorer for the first eleven. He closed his eyes. As President, there would be no further need to fear incurring the wrath of Nox, no need to fear his tongue and the direction it spread its venom. As President he would be once again in a position to overrule Nox when Nox got out of hand. As President he would have asked for Sanctuary's resignation a moment or two ago; in time he might well have to ask for it, and Nox's too, if the unfounded rumour about Dowse was not agreed to be a figment of Sanctuary's imagination. But waiting until the time came, waiting about, neither here nor there, curbing his speech so that he should not give offence – none of that suited him; it irritated, and made him feel almost imprisoned. He wished they had had the sense to make the decision at the last meeting, so that he knew where he stood.

Mr Jaraby slept and in his dream he was one of the flannelled figures at the wicket. Cricket had never been his game; he had always regretted his inability to reach high figures quickly, to bowl a deadly ball, neatly and to a length. Yet he had acquitted himself without disgrace. He had tried, and in turn he had received an adequate satisfaction. He was happier as a second-row forward, a forward who was not just one of the eight, but one who was out on his own: the pick of the pack. In his time Dowse's had won the House Cup four seasons running.

Jaraby's entry to the School had been, more or less, like everyone else's. He had suffered indignities similar to Nox's. He had fagged and been beaten, and lazed when he should have worked. Once when he was very new his fag-master sent him into the town to buy two pounds of sugar. On the way back he dropped the soft grey bag on the road; it burst and the sugar spilled, mingling with the dust. He spooned together as much as he could with his hands, but three-quarters was lost. He explained about it to his fag-master, who beat him first and then sent him back for more. His face was blotched and red as he trudged for the second time along the road. His body, in the process of development, was awkward and gangling; his gait, affected by the punishment, somewhat out of control. He hated the whole incident, the image of the torn paper-bag, his untidy efforts to clear up the mess, the set face of his fag-master as he learnt the news, the gesture with which he so casually reached for his cane, and the deft strokes with which he inflicted pain. Years afterwards Jaraby remembered the incident. When Nox was his fag, and others before and after Nox, he saw in retrospect the justice of what had happened to him. It was not difficult to see it thus, when justice might be justly passed on. Even as he returned to the shop for another two pounds of sugar he realized that he was there to accept such things, that he must learn to 'take it'. That was what he had not been able to teach Nox. Nox would not learn that his time would come, that for the moment he must simply 'take it' and live for the future, harbouring no grievance.

Mr Jaraby awoke, refreshed and lively. The scoreboard registered twenty-five for five, last man one.

'On the contrary,' said General Sanctuary, 'I think Jaraby would make an excellent President. He is just the sort of man to fill the position impeccably. Ponders is nicer but less efficient.'

Seeking an ally, Mr Nox was disappointed. Back in the environs of the School, so totally the scene of Jaraby's triumphs, his case seemed lost. Not that he had ever had one. The whole Swingler business was ridiculous; Swingler and the work he did were beneath contempt. Mr Nox felt ashamed of his own chicanery in employing the man. He would call Swingler off and would not see him again, since he disliked him so as a person. At this stage in his life he could at least choose with whom to associate.

Sanctuary, while obviously disapproving of Jaraby, would accept him as President. To Sanctuary he was just a clown. Mr Nox had not known that it was Dowse's practice to recommend brothels. Clearly – or it could be made to seem so – Jaraby had simply been passing information on; there was nothing to support an accusation that he had spoken from his own experience. It was perhaps a little odd that he had kept this address of Dowse's by him for half a century, but retaining an address of that nature hardly amounted to the picture of a reckless and disgraceful profligate that Mr Nox had hoped to paint. Abruptly he accepted defeat. He knew his limitations, and the knowledge hurt him; he could not see how he might ever now achieve victory. Jaraby remained top dog: it was still in the nature of things.

13

Mr Turtle stood alone by the bicycle sheds. They were sheds that had not been there in his time: he was trying to think what had stood in their place. A small boy was cleaning the handle-bars of a bicycle with a rag, taking advantage of the day of freedom.

Approaching the boy, Mr Turtle said: 'I broke my leg in this yard once.'

He looked around him, establishing the spot.

The boy paused in his labour, interested in the remark. He saw that at lunch something had spilled on Mr Turtle's waistcoat and left a white stain. He said: 'Are you an Old Boy, sir?'

He had slipped on a stick running to see if there was a letter for him. Somehow his foot had caught in the cobbles, and the weight of his falling body snapped the bone in his leg. 'It was in plaster for nearly a whole term. I almost had to learn how to walk with it again.'

'Wigg broke something, sir, at his prep school. I think he said a collar-bone.'

'It is easy to break the collar-bone.'

Why should they interfere with his life like this? Why should they talk against Miss Burdock? What business was it of anyone's but his that he was getting married? Old men got married, no one prevented them. Did they know better than he what it was like to have Mrs Strap coming to the house every morning, grumbling about the marks of his walking-stick on the linoleum? Did they know what it was to be always escaping from the images in his mind, and seeking people to talk to in parks?

'On Sundays, sir, we can go out on our bikes. We can take sandwiches. Me and Wigg are going out on Sunday.'

'Is Wigg – is that your great friend?'

'Oh, yes, sir. Wigg's father has a Mercedes-Benz. And a horse called Lightning. They're very rich, but the old horse never wins anything.'

'What's – what's the other thing you said?'

'A Mercedes-Benz? Don't you know, sir? It's a German car. It's probably the finest car in the world. It's very fast. I've been in it when it's gone a hundred miles an hour. On the M.1.'

Mr Turtle said: 'You would not reach that pace on your bicycle.' He smiled to show he knew he was making a joke.

'I don't think even a motor-cycle would, sir. No, I think a motor-cycle could go that fast. A motor-cycle can go as fast as a car, can't it, sir?'

'Oh, definitely, I think. Faster, you know.'

The boy nodded. Mr Turtle said: 'I had a great friend: Topham minor.' Topham had died a few years ago, after making a success of life. Mr Turtle was godfather to one of his sons. In his will there was a legacy for the younger Topham. 'I was keen on wild flowers when I was here.'

'Were you, sir? I'm quite good at carpentry. I made a bird-box last term. It's in the Junior Exhibition.'

'I did carpentry too; but I wasn't up to that standard. I don't remember ever having anything in an exhibition. I don't think there were any exhibitions.'

'We have a woodwork exhibition every year, sir. Mr Rathbone teaches us. Who taught you, sir?'

'Well now, d'you know, I can't remember that either. I think it was a little man with a moustache. It's a longish time ago.'

'Mr Rathbone has a beard. He teaches pottery as well; and archery. He's here today, sir, keeping an eye on the exhibitions.'

They shouldn't have spoken that way at lunch, discussing his private affairs in public. A total stranger had even become involved in the conversation. Why should they treat it so lightly, and laugh so much, as though he too treated it lightly and was marrying without thought or care? He enjoyed talking to Miss Burdock at the Rimini, he enjoyed going with her to the

97

Gaumont. Was that a crime? Was it a folly? Did they think he didn't know his own mind?

'It's a B.S.A., sir. I had it for my birthday, from my grandmother. My parents are in Kenya, sir.'

'I beg your pardon?'

'My parents are out in Kenya. I go to my grandmother's in the holidays. She lives in Totnes in Devon.'

Once he had gone to stay with Topham in Yorkshire. They had followed a river to its source, wading with their clothes tied to their heads. They must have looked odd, but Topham said that was the way to do it. Coming to the source was like reaching the peak of a mountain. Probably, he thought, it was one of the most exciting moments in his life.

'Kenya is a troublesome place these days.' The words slipped out: as soon as he spoke he was sorry he had said them.

'It's very beautiful, sir. Have you been there?'

'No, I've never been there. I've seen pictures, though.'

'Look, sir.' And the boy drew photographs from his wallet, of scenery and animals, of a house with children and adults in front of it.

'My mother's just had another baby. I haven't seen it yet, but I will this summer. I'm going out there.'

'You'll – you'll like that.'

'Yes, sir. It's funny having a sister you haven't seen.'

'Your mother is a very pretty lady.'

'She's photogenic, sir. I've got another sister, older than me. She goes to school in England too.'

'Do you know if it's half-past three?'

'A quarter to four, sir.'

'I must take a pill for my heart.'

'Yes, sir. Is that a bind, sir?'

'Well, I have to have them.'

'If you didn't, sir, what would happen? Would your heart stop altogether? Would you die, sir?'

'Probably. I have to lead a very quiet life, no excitement.'

'Wigg says they can take your heart out and put it back again.'

'Not, I imagine, if it's in poor shape like mine is.'

'I wouldn't like to have it done to me. The heart isn't the seat of affections, is it, sir?'

'I've heard it said the kidneys are. I think you know more than I do.'

'It's Wigg really, sir. His father tells him. Like what would happen if you laid all the railway lines in the world end to end all the way to the moon.'

'If you laid all the railway lines end to –'

'We'd have to go everywhere by car. D'you think that bike looks clean?'

'Very clean. Spotless.'

'Would you like to see my bird-box in the Exhibition?'

'What? Your –? Yes, yes, I would.'

'I'll just put the bicycle away.'

She had told him her Christian name and asked him to call her by it, but he couldn't for the moment remember what it was. Agnes? Agatha? Angela? Helen?

The boy returned from the bicycle shed. They walked to the Exhibition.

'That's Mr Rathbone, sir. The man with the beard. There's my bird-box.'

'Well, that seems finely made. Did you do it all yourself?'

'Mr Rathbone helped me a bit. You lift up the top to put the bread in, and that hole at the side is for the birds to go in and out. It's got to be just the right size; if it's too big they won't use it. Would you like to meet Mr Rathbone?'

'Yes, of course.'

'Mr Rathbone. Sir, this is –'

'Turtle the name is.'

'Sir, this is Mr Turtle. He's an Old Boy. Mr Turtle did woodwork too, sir.'

'How d'you do?' said Mr Rathbone, shaking hands.

'Quite a display,' Mr Turtle said.

'We do our best, you know. Some good stuff the older boys turn out. You interested in woodwork, sir?'

'Well, it was just that this young man –' Mr Turtle looked round for the boy.

'He trotted off,' Mr Rathbone said.

'A polite boy. Very nice. You don't often get that at that age.'

'We do our best with them. Not the same class of boy at all, of course. Still, *tempora mutantur*, as the Classics have it.'

'Sorry?'

'Just a reflection in passing, sir.'

'What?'

'The type of boy has changed since your day.'

'Oh. Well, I must trot off myself. Are you tied to your, hmm, stalls? Would you join me in a cup of tea?'

'I am tied, I fear. Some kind lad may fetch me a cup if I'm lucky.' Mr Rathbone laughed and they shook hands again. Mr Turtle, who had been fingering a sixpence to give to the boy, felt sorry that he was gone.

Tea was laid out in a large marquee, the property of a catering company. There was chocolate cake and shortbread, sandwiches, biscuits, and plates of raspberries and cream. The tea itself was of poor quality, metallic like rust water. It gushed from great tarnished urns that hissed and steamed menacingly. There were bowers of summer flowers against the canvas, tall delphiniums, roses and early asters. The Headmaster's wife fussed about, a nuisance to the caterers.

'Cake, Mr Turtle?' she cried, proud that she remembered his name. 'Chocolate cake with a thick filling? Or something else? There is lemon for that tea if you would rather.'

Mr Turtle took tea and cake. The woman was right, the filling was thick and good. Should he give her the sixpence, he wondered, to pass on to the boy? He remembered the boy's face quite well; it would not be difficult to describe. But the Headmaster's wife was talking to someone else.

He stood alone, drinking from a flowered cup, watching the

marquee fill with people and voices. He and Topham used to hang round the marquee on Old Boys' Day, waiting to slip in at the end of tea and take what remained of the cakes and the raspberries. Probably it was the same marquee, or at least of the same vintage: marquees are made to last. It would be nice to be talking to Topham today, as Cridley had Sole to talk to and Sole had Cridley. They weren't aware of it but they guarded their friendship a bit. He had felt too grateful when they invited him to journey with them today. When one needed friendship, now or as a boy, there were always difficulties like that.

A woman in a white overall broke in on his thoughts, pressing a plate of wafer biscuits on him. He sighed and smiled and took one. How nice it would be to hear a bell and run to its summons, to join a queue for milk or cocoa, and later to do prep and wait for another bell that meant the rowdy security of the dormitory. How nice it would be to slip, tired and a little homesick, between the cold sheets. He heard his name called. Somebody gave him a fresh cup of tea and asked him a question he did not understand.

14

At four o'clock, as Mr Jaraby was taking his first spoonful of rasp-berries and cream, Mrs Jaraby was offering sleeping pills to his cat. She had given Monmouth nothing to eat all day. Breaking the pills, four times the recommended adult dose, she mixed them into a plate of fish, knowing that they would be instantly and carelessly consumed. They were. Monmouth lay in a stupor on the kitchen floor, the empty eye-socket wide and sinister, flakes of fish lingering on his fur. Mrs Jaraby poked him with the end of a broom. She poked harder; she placed her foot on his tail and gradually brought the weight of her body to bear. The cat did not wake up. Mrs Jaraby fetched a sack.

Monmouth was heavy and unwieldy, and Mrs Jaraby had diffi-culty in getting him into the sack. She wore gloves, removing them only to tie the mouth of the sack with a piece of string. She dragged the burden upstairs, panting with every step. Once she thought she felt the animal move, and stood back in terror in case he should tear his way to liberty. She stood at the top of the stairs, looking down at the sack, which was about half-way up. There was no movement now; she hauled it up the remaining steps, across the landing, over the smooth surface of the bathroom floor. She paused then, looking from the sack to the bath three-quarters full of water. Straining herself, she raised the sack from the floor and toppled it as gently as she could over the side. She had to wedge it beneath the surface of the water with a chair.

At half-past five Mrs Jaraby returned to the bathroom, laid an old macintosh coat of her husband's on the floor, removed the chair from the bath and bundled the sack over the edge. She folded the coat about it, tying it in place with string. She pulled it from the bathroom, allowing its own weight to carry it down the stairs. From the hall she dragged it through the kitchen into the backyard. She had removed the contents of a dustbin and placed the bin ready on its side. She shoved the sack in, levered the dustbin into an upright position again, covered the sack with tins, newspapers and potato peelings, and replaced the lid.

Mrs Jaraby let the water out of the bath, cleaned away the scum, and set the house to rights. She put a hat on, took some money from her purse and walked to the bus-stop. She could have sent the telegram over the telephone, but she preferred to see the message in writing. She wrote in her spidery handwriting with a difficult post office pen. The ink ran into the absorbent paper, but the girl behind the counter was able to read it; Mrs Jaraby made sure of that.

Your birds no longer threatened. Monmouth died today. Come as you wish. Love. Mother.

15

The portrait of H. L. Dowse, part of a gallery of housemasters of note, hung in the Dining Hall. Eyeing it, Mr Nox wondered if what Sanctuary had said was true. There was certainly nothing in the portrait to lend credence to his claim, yet one would hardly expect that there should be. The Headmaster was making a speech, thanking the Old Boys for their contribution to the new classroom block. Mr Jaraby wished he could make a speech too, with a couple of barbed remarks in it about the architecture. Sir George Ponders, who was about to make a speech, wished he wasn't.

'Of course, of course.' Mr Sole expressed surprise when Mr Jaraby had questioned him about the presidency. 'I am surprised you ask me: naturally you shall have my vote. And Cridley's. I can vouch for Cridley.' And Mr Sole had gone on to say that in his opinion Mr Jaraby would be elected without opposition.

Applause was given by beating the table with one's right hand. Some of the younger Old Boys, who had slipped down to the town between Reunion Service and dinner, were beating the tables with their brandy glasses, a couple of them with spoons. Far away in the Headmaster's dining-room a dozen wives were listening to the Headmaster's wife talking about domestic staff problems.

Mr Jaraby had made his annual round of old haunts. He had been introduced to a couple of new masters, had had a glass of sherry with one whom he had known for years, had talked to the editor of the School magazine and discussed with the Captain of Games the fixture list for next term. Earlier in the afternoon he had noticed Turtle wandering about the place with a small boy and had seen Cridley and Sole sitting at desks in a classroom, pretending they were back at school.

'You won't forget our last committee meeting, Turtle? Dinner too.' Mr Turtle had promised not to forget. Mr Jaraby was to be the next President; Mr Turtle took it for granted. He said so twice.

General Sanctuary was thinking he would rather go on drinking brandy in his hotel than watch the Dramatic Society's production of *The Mikado*. He had seen too many productions of *The Mikado*, he was tone-deaf anyway.

The Headmaster rambled on rather, then Sir George spoke and no one could hear what he said. He lost his place a few times and had to keep going back to the beginning of the paragraph, but nobody noticed because nobody could hear.

'May I count on you, Sanctuary? May I count on you to back me as President, eh?' But General Sanctuary had said: 'Good heavens, what an extraordinary question to ask!' and had walked away, whistling.

Although it was still light, the heavily leaded windows of the Dining Hall necessitated the use of electricity. The tall, narrow windows were dark and uncurtained. When the sun fell on them it revealed scenes in stained glass of a mundane and familiar kind; profane rather than sacred. But the sun did not reach them now; here and there a dusty red gleamed, or an inky blue, little spurts of colour in a total gloom. The rest of the great hall was merry enough: tobacco smoke curled towards the high beams of the ceiling, decanters littered the tables. The House Cups and the silver had been polished for the occasion; there was an air of celebration and bonhomie; the panelling glowed, the human faces shone. The nostalgia that was present was certainly not for meals taken as a boy; rather it related to other Old Boys' Days and other reunions. Remembered now was the moment at this very dinner when a maid had dropped a silver tray of walnuts on the floor; and when a young man from the Middle East had abruptly leapt on to a table and harangued his audience, demanding British troops for his country.

Mr Turtle over his brandy felt nostalgic in his own way, and tipsy as well. They were right, he didn't know his own mind. He would see Miss Burdock and explain. He must explain that one is too indecisive and absurd for marriage at his age. In these familiar surroundings he could not see why he had ever proposed marriage to her. Had he done so? Was it just some joke of Sole's and Cridley's? He had gone to the pictures with her and had lost his shoe; he had gone to the pictures again, and afterwards they had had tea in a café. But he couldn't remember what they had talked about. He couldn't remember the name of the young man in the park, the young man whom he had met again on the same seat and to whom he had lent a little more money. He had gone to see the man's birds and had listened while he spoke about them. He would still have liked to have had one, but when finally he mentioned it to Mrs Strap she was angry, as he knew she would be. He knew the man's house, he would visit him again, and talk to him about Mrs Strap. Perhaps the man, who was younger and abler than he, would speak to Mrs Strap about the bird. Perhaps, even, he would help him to find another Mrs Strap, a Mrs Strap who was not always going on and who did not always want to see his will. He might become quite interested in the bird and have others. He might visit the young man quite often and have the young man drop in on him unexpectedly. Hadn't he said that he too was an Old Boy? Hadn't he said so, and could not manage the membership fee? He could help him over the fee; perhaps next year they would come to the Old Boys' Day together. Was it in the café he had proposed to Miss Burdock? She had worn something at her neck, a brooch with a dog on it. Miss Burdock, Mrs Strap: between them, like animals, they would tear whatever was left of him apart. His bones would crack, his flesh would fall away, his blood would be grey, hardened to powder in his arteries. He felt afraid, he thought he might already have gone too far along a destined course and that now there was no chance of turning back. He began to weep, and the man next to him nudged his shoulder, thinking maybe that weeping was like falling asleep.

'Excuse me,' said Mr Jaraby. 'I've been trying to have a word with you all day.'

The man he approached was twenty years his junior, a man with half a cigar in his mouth, and spectacles and smooth grey hair brushed back from his temples.

'I'm Jaraby. Look, shall we take a stroll beneath the elms? I'd appreciate a word of advice.'

'Certainly, Mr Jaraby,' said the man, smiling, and swearing inwardly.

'Now you're a medical man,' Mr Jaraby told him. 'You know – I'm sorry, your name escapes me.'

'Mudie.'

'Well, it's really – look, Mudie, I'd welcome a word of professional advice about my wife.'

'Oh dear, I'm afraid –'

Mr Jaraby held up his hand. 'This is quite serious. Our own doctor is long in the tooth, behind the times, against modern methods, you know the kind of thing. Now I think you as an Old Boy would be prepared –'

'Mr Jaraby, what is the trouble with your wife? If you are dissatisfied with your own doctor you should change. It is quite a simple thing to do.'

'Yes, yes, but I'd rather do this on a man-to-man basis, if you follow me. It's an awkward and embarrassing case, not easy to explain to a stranger. You and I, as it were, belong to the same club, speak the same language. I am more confident with a man of your calibre.'

'Perhaps if you told me –'

'This is all in confidence, mind. Strictly in confidence. I would not like this to be noised abroad.'

'All that concerns a patient is confidential, Mr Jaraby. But I must warn you this may be a fruitless conversation. Mrs Jaraby is not my patient. I may not be able to help at all.'

'My wife is touched, Mudie.'

'Touched?'

'Touched in the head. A bit odd. Mad if you like.'

'I see.'

'She will sit in a room with the television on but the sound turned off. For instance she might be watching a play. She will then turn on the wireless.'

'Yes?'

'One play on the television, one on the wireless, and she will attempt to match the voices on the wireless with the figures on the television.'

'I see.'

'It is pitiful to see.'

'Are there other signs of your wife's unrest?'

'My dear fellow, a ton of signs. She has invited a near-criminal back to the house after an absence of fifteen years. Between them they will fill the house with birds. She imagines the cat is a tiger. She speaks constantly of the hand of Death. There is madness in her family.'

'If there is madness in her family –'

'Her mother and father both, very queer people. Now dead of course. I fear for my son, you see. He is a deep, strange fellow with hardly a word to say for himself. Frankly, Mudie, if my son came back to live at Crimea Road I should immediately have to have both of them looked at.'

'I am sorry to hear all this, Mr Jaraby. But I'm afraid there is absolutely nothing I can do.'

'What I would like from you, Mudie, is pills to quieten her. Some gentle sedative she would take every day. I would have to put them in food, she would not cooperate at all. But if I could have something that would bring a little peace to the house . . .'

'You have seen Mrs Jaraby's doctor?'

'A useless fellow, Mudie. I've seen him and argued and pleaded.

I've left no stone unturned. I'm coming to you as a last resort. I'm sorry on a day like this to bother you, but the thing is on my mind.'

'Yes, I can see it is a worry. But, you know, apart from imagining the cat is a tiger, I cannot see from what you have told me that Mrs Jaraby is unhinged in any way. Of course, one would have to examine her.'

'No point. No point at all. She is up to every little trick and would be on her best behaviour.'

'I could give you the name of a good man your wife might see.'

'She would see no one. She does not go out except for shopping, which is another thing she has fallen asunder over.'

'I beg your pardon?'

'She brings outrageous produce into the house. Look, Mudie, I cannot go into all these details. The simplest thing of all is for you to write me out a prescription.'

'That, I'm afraid, is not possible.'

'Are there not good homes where a woman like that would be well looked after? It may come to that, I may yet be left to linger out my days alone. What would the process be to get her a bed?'

'You are putting me in an awkward position, Mr Jaraby. I should not be discussing this at all. Let me give you the name of a man you might see.'

'Come yourself, Mudie. Come yourself to tea one day. I will not say who you are, beyond being an Old Boy of the School. You will see how the land lies, and may feel bound to issue a certificate.'

'I don't know that I much care for that idea.'

'Look, come to tea, man-to-man. Give me an opinion afterwards. No obligation. Let's say I issue the invitation in return for this unorthodox consultation. How's that then? I am bending over backwards to accommodate you.'

'It is very kind of you, Mr Jaraby. But I have not helped you at all; you must not feel it necessary to invite me to your house as payment.'

'Come on Saturday, four p.m. Ten Crimea Road. A number eighty-one bus.'

'It is very civil of you –'

'It is also time for *The Mikado*,' laughed Mr Jaraby.

Mr Sole, Mr Cridley and Mr Turtle sat together. They could see the peak of Fujiyama and the occasional sinister Japanese mien, but to see more they were obliged to stretch themselves this way and that, in reverse time to similar movements on the part of the person in front. Familiarity with the plot, however, allowed them to relax, and microphones carried the sound at a magnified pitch. At the end of the second act Mr Cridley said:

'Turtle talked to himself all during the first bit and slept during the second. There wasn't much point in his coming.'

'She's on his mind.'

'A pretty thought, God wot. He must set sail at once for Yalta, before it's too late.'

'She'd have him for breach of promise. Wake the old fool up. What's done cannot be undone.'

But Mr Sole was wrong. For Mr Turtle, who had slept peacefully through the second act, had died peacefully at the end of it.

Once when he was seven years old Basil had taken a nail from an open counter in Woolworth's. The nail was no good to him, he had no use for it, and afterwards he threw it away. But taking it, slipping his fingers up over the glass edge and snatching the nail into the palm of his hand, that had delighted him. It delighted him even more than he knew; and he didn't guess then that taking the nail from Woolworth's was the real beginning of his furtive life.

As he stood in the centre of his room, his stomach twitching with anxiety, he remembered the purloining of the nail. He was thinking that he should have told the woman about it. He should have tried to explain to her that bringing her little girl to see his birds was another action of the same kind; that his life had been constructed of actions like that; that he meant no harm at all. And the little girl hadn't been frightened. She had done what he had asked her to do, and only afterwards – when he had led her back to the playground in the park, fearing that she might not know her way; when her mother had shouted at her and at him – only then had she said that she was afraid. But the mother said her clothes were torn, which was true because she had torn them herself, snatching the child from his hand. The mother had said that she would go with her husband to the police, and then in her fear the child was suddenly on the mother's side; and he knew that she would lead them to where he lived.

He spoke to the birds, explaining what had happened, and what must happen now. He sobbed for a while, and when he ceased the room was silent except for the sound of movement in the cages. Then Mrs Jaraby's telegram arrived.

General Sanctuary remembered Turtle at school, long-legged, thin, and good at the high jump. He tried to find out about the funeral, but nobody could tell him anything. He was sorry that Turtle was dead.

Mr Nox thought Turtle had been about to marry rather than die, and wondered how serious the former prognostication had been. Jaraby would live to a great age, Jaraby was made like that. So, he decided, would he.

'A bad business,' said Mr Sole, 'but all for the best in the long run.' Mr Cridley agreed. They looked forward to telling Miss Burdock.

Sir George Ponders reminded his wife that they had never had Mr Turtle to dinner. 'Poor old man,' said Lady Ponders. 'One thinks of these things too late. At least we can go to the funeral.'

Mr Swabey-Boyns, who had not been able to attend Old Boys' Day because of a stomach upset, tried to take the death philosophically but failed. 'I shall be next,' he murmured. 'I shall outlive no one now.' (In fact he was wrong. He outlived all his fellows on the committee. He died at ninety-two, nineteen years later, as a result of carelessness on the part of a man in a motor-car.)

Mr Jaraby was shocked by death. Turtle had worn badly. But someone should have seen what was happening and taken him out of the Assembly Hall. No one could wish to die during a performance of The Mikado.

Mrs Strap took Mr Turtle's will from his writing-desk and placed it in the centre of the dining-room table. She put a vase and a few pairs of scissors in a basket that already contained Mr Turtle's travelling clock. She hunted in drawers for cuff-links and other small pieces. Finding nothing that excited her, she returned to the will. *Amy Strap, for devoted services, one thousand pounds*. It was she who had suggested the word *devoted*. She would have preferred guineas, but Mr Turtle had not seemed to understand her when she mentioned it. She left the house with the basket and a table.

Turtle died during *The Mikado*. They had to scrap the last act.'

'Your cat too,' cried Mrs Jaraby. 'Returned to his Maker. And Basil back in residence.'

'What residence? What do you say?'

'Basil is with us again. He is above us now, cages of birds festoon the house. Hark, and you may hear them.'

'Is Basil here? With birds?'

'Be calm a moment. Sit down, compose yourself. Ask me question by question. The answers required vary.'

'It is you who should compose yourself. You are going on in a mad way. What is all this?'

'I am breaking news to you; why don't you listen?'

'What of Monmouth? Is Monmouth injured?'

'Injured unto death. Does that mean dead? It doesn't, does it? You missed the monster's passing.'

'Is Monmouth dead?'

'I have said so with variation.'

'Monmouth and Turtle too. My God, my God!'

'He is not just your God. "Our God, our God!" should be your cry.'

'For heaven's sake, do not make a joke now.'

'Shall we go into weeds? Is mourning the order of the day? Shall I stitch black bands to the arms of your jackets? Your style of conversation is catching: now I am asking the questions. Shall I ask them singly and get an answer?'

'You answer me, woman: what became of my cat?'

'Struck by a passing van, flattened beneath its wheels.'

'Struck? How was Monmouth killed? Did you observe the accident?'

'The foolish cat ran wild across the road. The thing was blind, you know. The van just mowed it down and proceeded on. The man was unaware.'

'So Monmouth is dead.'

'He was out of hand, dominating our life as he did. The house will be happier without him.'

'I have known Monmouth for fourteen years.'

'You nursed him when he lost an eye.'

'What became – where is he now?'

'In some ash-tip, naturally we know not where. I collected the carcass on your garden spade and committed it to the dustbin. I knew you would not wish to leave the thing where it was. It was unsightly too.'

'Did you say – did you put Monmouth in a dustbin?'

'The men came this morning. The corpse is off the premises. You do not have the sadness of mulling over the body.'

'Did you put my cat in a dustbin?'

'Did I not say so? I am not given to idle prevarications.'

'A cat should have respect, as a human. I would have wished to bury my cat in the garden.'

'With last rites? Shall we recover the flattened victim and have a vicar call? Was Monmouth Christian?'

'Don't go too far. I warn you, I have already taken steps to bring this folly to an end. I question a savage action: a dead cat, an old and loved pet, incarcerated in a dustbin. I do not suggest last rites or vicars. To have made a simple mound with my hands in my own garden – is that an unnatural thing?'

'It is pure sentiment. Slop and fiddlesticks. The cat had had his innings. He is gone, thank God, and that is that.'

'The same applies to Turtle, does it? Slop and sentiment is it, to feel sorrow at an old man's grave?'

'I did not say that. Do you expect me to weep and tear my hair over an elderly man I have never met? I would not put Mr Turtle's body in a dustbin, if by chance you are thinking that.'

'You put poor Monmouth's, a creature you have known for fourteen years. You could not care that the man you did not know should end likewise. Do not pretend; actions reveal your nature.'

'You are on to a faulty argument. You must bring it to its apt conclusion: would you mete out to Mr Turtle what was Monmouth's due, a mound in your garden created by hand? Would you delve thus for the man as for the cat? You claim I see the deaths as equal. Would you be as affectionate over the man as you say I would be cruel?'

'Turtle's place now is the cemetery, Monmouth's our garden. That is the natural order of things. No man buries his life's friends in his garden. This talk of yours disturbs me.'

'It is you who bring such talk to the surface. You imply I approve of human remains on an ash-tip. I invest you with the sweeter thought: the burial of a friend with your own hands. How can you object to that?'

'I object to your callous treatment of my cat. Have you ever cared for a pet? Cannot you see how I must feel?'

'You feel disgust maybe, as I have felt over the cat's murdering ways. You may this minute strip yourself of your good clothes and build a million mounds in the garden, marking them with crosses to signify what the cat in fourteen years has killed. Why not do that to ease your mind?'

'You are mocking my sorrow. I am brought low by sudden deaths and you jest and jeer, since you are made that way. Have you no word of comfort?'

'I have made practical suggestions. Act on them and you may find relief. As to pets, there are new pets now in the house; you need not feel cut off from the animal kingdom.'

'What pets are new? How can I understand if you speak in this way? You make no sense at all.'

'I speak only repetitively. I have already said there are eight new coloured birds in cages. They are bred as pets, bought and sold in millions.'

'Why is Basil here? If he has brought this circus with him, then he and it must go at once. I did not give any consent, I did not invite him.'

'Your son replaces your cat. You leave in the house an animal, you return to welcome a human form. It is almost a fairy story.'

'Basil shall not live here again. On that I am adamant.'

'You may cease to be adamant, for Basil is here already. He is well entrenched and happy in his old room.'

'I shall speak to him. I shall speak man-to-man. He knows my wishes.'

'If he knows your wishes, then there is no need surely to speak, man-to-man or otherwise. He doesn't care for your wishes.'

'I am defied in my own house. I leave it for a day and a night and return to this chaos.'

'Life replaces death; you must be glad of that. There is no chaos, just the simple order of a family. We each have a part to play in the future and must not interfere. There is Basil in his room, I am in mine, you are in yours. We meet in the more general rooms and honour, if we have to, another point of view. We must stick to civilized arrangements.'

'You are telling me. You are laying down the law, usurping my position. It is up to me to say yea or nay, to send this shabby man packing. I have the right to protest at a menagerie brought into my house when my back is turned.'

'Possession is nine points of the law. You may well have to employ the final point to eject your son.'

'You know of Basil's past. You know we washed our hands long since of him. By accepting him now we are adding a blessing to his dishonesties.'

'What has he ever done? You speak of your son as though he had taken charge of a gas chamber.'

'He has left hotels with bills unpaid; he has borrowed indiscriminately from strangers; passed cheques that were worthless.

How many times have I had to pay double the amount to quieten creditors?'

'A few seaside hotels where he was temporarily a little short. A bishop might be short of money and seek aid in his predicament. What is a father for, if not for that? If you make some instrument that damages others you are surely responsible for it? Responsibility for a son comes by the same token.'

'One is not for a lifetime responsible for one's mistakes.'

'You are wrong. You blow all this up like a balloon. Who has not borrowed money? It is easy to miscalculate a cheque-book.'

'It is not a passing error that one uses a cheque-book one has no right to use, of a bank in which one has never deposited money.'

'You are fuzzy about the facts. You are determined to see Basil in a certain light. You embroider and exaggerate.'

'Good God, the facts are facts, as clear as day. You speak as though I were a child.'

'I speak to you as you are: an old man whose memory is imperfect, who rejects a failed son and determines his sins. You cannot see the larger issue. You are lost amongst the trees, while the pattern of the wood holds the secret. Do not shirk your natural responsibility.'

'I shirk nothing. I have faced more than most men, and now I am to face it all afresh. How do we know the birds are not stolen? Has our house become a thieves' kitchen overnight? We may be some kind of receivers.'

'You must ask Basil outright if the birds are stolen. Since that worries you, seek assurance. I cannot imagine the stealing of birds. It would not be easy, you know.'

'He is adept at that kind of thing. He is well trained in thieving. He will have things from the house.'

'Then we must lock away our valuables and be on our guard. That is not beyond me. Though I think it would be less troublesome to ask Basil to leave our things alone. Shall you do that, since you brought the subject up?'

'I shall be silent,' cried Mr Jaraby. 'I shall not utter a word of any kind to Basil. My displeasure shall take that form.'

'You could not be silent. You have never been silent all your life. Pass the time of day with Basil. Take an interest in his hobby. Be kind, and you and he may be the better for it.'

'I shall do as I please. Why should I be kind, or take an interest in flights of birds? I am not kindly disposed to him, I see no point in birds. He does no honest work, he does not toil as the rest of society. He has come home to roost like a parasite.'

'Parasites do not roost. But you are right to say he has come home. That is the case in a nutshell. The prodigal returns, we celebrate graciously. Can you manage that?'

'No, I can not manage that. I feel no sense of celebration, only foreboding. Too much has happened in twenty-four hours, I cannot take it in.'

'Shall I cover the ground again? Shall we make notes on a piece of paper to help you? Your Mr Turtle dies and is carried from the audience, a cat gives up the ghost, the son with birds returns. I will tell you more, go further into detail, of how the cat looked like a tiger hearth-rug on the road, of Basil's arrival with the cages in a taxi-cab. I gave him tea and aspirin.'

'I do not wish to hear all this. It adds nothing. Was it a familiar van? Did the man apologize?'

'The van drove on. It is not against the law to kill a cat, though the death of a dog must be reported. If you would like to speak of Mr Turtle's death I will listen to oblige you.'

'Why should you listen? You are not interested.'

'To talk things over is often a help.'

'Why should I talk things over? The man died. You are after some morbid details and you shall not have them. The man died and people were shocked. Is there more to be said?'

'That is up to you. Say more and I will listen. Reel off an obituary that I may know more of the subject and come to feel shocked too. He may have welcomed death, in which case to be shocked is hypocrisy.'

'Poor Monmouth! I cannot even count on you to keep an eye on him while I am away.'

'In Monmouth's case, it's an ill wind that blows no good. For though you are saddened, I rejoice.'

'How can you rejoice when my cat has died?'

'Because he will leave no more hairs about the house, nor ends of fish to be trodden into the carpets and rot and smell.'

'Is that your respect for the dead?'

'Can you hear the birds? Prepare yourself for your son.'

18

'An old man, Turtle, has died,' Mrs Jaraby said. 'The event has taken a toll of your father.' And Basil thought that he owed Mr Turtle fifteen pounds ten and would owe him no more. Mr Turtle had been going to buy a bird, had even picked one out.

'Why did he die?'

'Your father did not say. God called him maybe, as God called Monmouth on the same day.'

Mr Jaraby sat without speaking, picked at the lunch on his plate.

Basil had not shaved. He thought it wise to let his beard grow for a while and perhaps do something about the colour of his hair.

'Your father is not himself. These Old Boys' occasions are tiring, exposed like that to the sun all day. Why do women not make a fuss about their schooldays?'

Basil took lettuce and radishes, remembering Old Boys' Days when he had been at school.

'There is more in a woman's life I suppose,' Mrs Jaraby went on. 'Women are often more sensible than men.'

'So you are living in the house.' Mr Jaraby spoke with his head bent over his plate, his eyes on the food.

'I have lived here for forty years,' said Mrs Jaraby. 'In the room next to yours.'

'I am speaking to Basil, as well you know. You are hellbent on trouble today, and you will find the reward is not pretty. You are living in the house, Basil?'

'I came yesterday, in the evening.'

'Did I issue the invitation when you came to tea? My memory fails me, I had quite forgotten.'

'I can vouch for you,' Mrs Jaraby cried. 'I stood beside you at the time. You invited Basil, I clapped and cheered you.'

'You are telling a lie, woman.'

'How can you know? You say your memory has gone!'

'I know my emotions, I know what I do and say or do not do and say.'

'After lunch, sleep in the garden. You will be clearer in your mind when you awake. We must not tax ourselves too much. We have to get used to this and that before we can operate properly again.'

'What in God's name are you talking about now? Are you simply using words because they are there and you can call upon them? All our conversation is like that. A yes and a no and a thank you are all I require from you. I ask you to note that, and act upon it.'

'I must note it since I have heard it. To act upon it is another thing. I ask you to note that I do not intend to act upon it.'

'You serve us with lettuce that is foul and coarse. One day in the year you have to order the lettuce and this is what we get. Do you not find the lettuce inedible, Basil?'

'Basil has eaten his lettuce without noticing anything amiss. There was not much wrong with today's lettuce. You bought it yourself.'

'How could I have? I have been away.'

'You have not been away for a year. You bought it the day before yesterday. I saw it was a little shot, but did not worry much. Rightly as it turned out, for it tasted –'

'I deny that I bought this lettuce. It was your doing on my day of absence.'

'You make too much of it. We are lucky to have food at all.'

'Lucky – why are we lucky? What do you mean we are lucky to have food?'

'If we were starving you would not make this fuss about a head of lettuce.'

Basil rose and left the table, shambling from the room and lighting a cigarette in the doorway.

'The lettuce has been paid for. We have a right to it, and a right to a better quality than this. We are not starving, and certainly in my present troubles I do not consider myself lucky.'

'We have exhausted the subject of the lettuce. You tell me to answer you simply with a yes or a no, and then you start a complicated discussion of a lettuce. You are not consistent.'

'I am consistent in this: I do not like that man lighting cigarettes in the house. I do not like him in the house at all. Did you see how he addressed me? Hardly listening to what I asked, surly and ill-tempered.'

'You did not meet his eye. What did you expect in return?'

'He has always been a trouble. As a child he was never off the sick-bed.'

'That was because he was sick. Should we have given him away when we discovered that? Should we have sold him to the highest bidder?'

'Did I say that? You are putting words into my mouth.'

'Are they words that displease you as much as the lettuce? They should not, for the thought has been in your mind.'

'To sell my son? You are mad. I have never thought of selling – this is a ridiculous conversation.'

'All our conversations are ridiculous. We speak without communication.'

'Am I to blame? Other people understand me. In my public life I am a success.'

Mrs Jaraby laughed. 'You are past public life now. Did you have a public life once? I had not noticed.'

'By public life I mean my life outside this house. There is, for instance, my contribution to the Association. Does that count for naught in your estimation? Are you above such matters?'

'I imagine your contribution was a worthy one; certainly your interest never flagged. Would that you had shown similar interest within the house, or made as worthy a contribution.'

'What do you mean by that?'

'The house might fall about our ears, you would not notice.

You cannot erect a shelf or undertake a simple home repair. You trim the garden now and then, but the very floors might rot beneath our feet before you cared. With time on your hands, I would have thought to see you painting skirting-boards and papering rooms; helping me in my daily chores.'

'I am not an artisan, I know nothing of such things. I cannot drive a nail or saw wood: I do not wish to: I might have mastered the crafts but chose not to. The house is in fair condition; I see nothing to complain at.'

'You would lead a more useful life now had you mastered these crafts you sneer at. You would throw some of your energy into healthy pursuits.'

'Are my present pursuits not healthy then? Let us hear all you have to say.'

'You have no pursuits. You do nothing. You have come to a full stop.'

'I help to keep the Association going. I organized collections for the new classroom block. I am in communication with thousands –'

'I know, I know. But what is that? A clerk could do it. What you do, you do for your own ends. You do not care a fig for that school. You use it and its association of Old Boys as your audience, for your display of power. You are lost if you cannot persuade yourself that you still have power. You will become President because you have paved the way. You are interested only in yourself, Mr Jaraby. You are still proving yourself in your own eyes.'

'You decrepit old fool,' cried Mr Jaraby in great anger, 'I have never heard such poppycock.'

Mrs Jaraby stood up. Her long angular figure towered over him and he felt for a moment a spark of fear, for her thin hands were like claws and her eyes, he thought, had the light of a vulture.

'I am not a fool,' Mrs Jaraby said. 'I am a sad, pathetic woman whose life has dropped into shreds. Basil shall remain in this house. He shall cram it from top to bottom with budgerigars and parrots and owls and eagles. He shall turn your garden into a tank for fish and train lizards to sing before your eyes. If he wishes for penguins and hyenas they shall be welcome. And the swift gazelle and the ostrich and the kangaroo. No matter what we do or what we now consent to we shall owe him a debt as we die. His birth was a greater sin than ever he in his wretchedness committed. I take my share of it. You, even at this advanced time, have not the confidence to take yours.'

'I will have you certified,' cried Mr Jaraby. 'As God is my Maker, I will have you certified.'

'Check first that He was your Maker.' Mrs Jaraby laughed shrilly and pulled a face at him, and watched him thinking that she was mad.

In his room Basil lay on his bed. He had pulled the curtains, for like Mr Swabey-Boyns he disliked the sun. In the gloom, cigarette ash spilled over his waistcoat and on to the sheets. He was thinking of Mr Turtle, that old man, now dead and awaiting burial. Mr Turtle had invited him to his house and given him money. Mr Turtle had listened while he talked to him about the birds, explaining their illnesses and their needs. He had said a bird would be a companion for him and had spoken then of the difficulties he faced in a domestic way. Once, as they sat together in the park, a young man in running attire had darted by, trailing a pungent exhaust of sweat, and Mr Turtle told him how once he had broken the high jump record. Basil did not as a rule wish to hear the School mentioned, but somehow he didn't mind when Mr Turtle went on about the high jump. He remembered the old man's hands and the stick with a silver knob and the story about Mr Turtle's marriage. Mr Turtle had suggested that some day they should go to a matinée at the cinema together, and Basil had agreed, because he knew that Mr Turtle would be the one to pay, and afterwards he knew that they would have tea. It was odd how when first he had met him he thought of him purely as a possible source of money, and had only later seen that he might become a friend. Had the relationship been a little more advanced, and had

Mr Turtle not died, he might even have gone to his house rather than his parents'. He had thought before of going to Mr Turtle's house, of offering to take the place of the difficult woman, of living there and cleaning the place and cooking for both of them. He had thought he might suggest it, and that Mr Turtle would be pleased and enthusiastic and might leave him the house in his will. Basil closed his eyes, blinking away the tears. They rolled down his cheeks into the dark stubble of his one-day beard.

19

When Dr Mudie rang the bell of 10 Crimea Road, the door was eventually opened by a bespectacled middle-aged man with dyed blond hair and a short black beard.

'I am looking for Mr Jaraby.' As he spoke, it seemed to Dr Mudie that the man made a half-hearted attempt to close the door again.

'Actually,' Basil said, 'I am Jaraby.'

'Surely not.' Dr Mudie looked closer. There was no doubt at all that the figure before him was featuring a crude disguise, but it was equally clear to Dr Mudie that this was not Jaraby. Could it be, he wondered, that Jaraby, far from exaggerating, had understated the case; that the wife in question was given to dressing up in male clothes, with wigs and beards?

Basil identified Dr Mudie as a person with sinister intent: a stranger at the door asking for Mr Jaraby meant a stranger with official purpose: guilt lay behind the assumption that he himself was the Jaraby required. 'There is no Jaraby here': that was what, with time to compose himself, he should have said at once; that was the reply that was more in line with his growth of beard and the colour of his hair. He saw the man penetrate his disguise and felt again the ticking of fear in his stomach.

'We are at cross purposes,' Dr Mudie went on. 'I think it must be your father I have come to see.'

'My father?'

'The elder Mr Jaraby. He invited me to tea.' Dr Mudie was a humane man; he saw this journey to the suburbs as a humane gesture. But he had also expected some kind of welcome. By the look of things, his host was not even present.

'Is your father here? I think it is the right day, Saturday four o'clock?'

'I can't say whether he is here or not. I don't know. The house seems quiet.'

'Perhaps you could find that out? May I come in?'

Dr Mudie entered and observed a tall woman in black descending the stairs. 'Is it a man about birds?' she called to her son.

Basil did not seem to hear. He took a package of cigarettes from his pocket and lit one, standing in the hall with Dr Mudie.

'May I introduce myself?' Dr Mudie requested. 'I am Dr Mudie. The elder Mr Jaraby invited me to tea. You must be Mrs Jaraby.' He stretched out a hand and grasped one of Mrs Jaraby's.

'The elder Mr Jaraby? But he is not here. He has gone to the shops. He did not mention a teatime guest.'

'In that case I must retrace my steps,' said Dr Mudie, a trifle piqued.

'Oh, never go,' cried Mrs Jaraby. 'What do you require?'

'Well, tea, I suppose. But it is far better for me to go away. Mr Jaraby has clearly forgotten.'

'No, no. Come in. Devoted couple that we are, a friend of my husband's is a friend of mine. May I present my son Basil? Dr Mudie, your father's chum.'

They were in the sitting-room, hovering about the seats by the open french windows. 'Sit down, sit down. Entertain him, Basil, while I prepare a meal.'

'I really do feel this is an imposition,' Dr Mudie said. 'Coming here like this.'

'Who did you say you were?'

'Mudie. A medical doctor.'

'You came to see my father?'

'Actually he did invite me.'

'Is my father ill?'

'It is not your father – I was merely asked to come to tea. I ran across him on Old Boys' Day. I say, were you at the School? I have had this at the back of my mind since you opened the door to me. Weren't we there together? Tell me I'm right. I never forget a face.'

'I don't remember you. I think you are mistaken. My face has altered.'

'Jaraby, B. Wasn't there some trouble over table manners?'

Basil did not reply. Driven to silence, Dr Mudie examined the ornaments.

'The fare is meagre,' Mrs Jaraby announced. 'Blackberry jelly in sandwiches. I trust you did not come with more in mind?'

'Delicious. Your son and I have established that we were fellows together at school, at least of the same generation.'

'Are you an Old Boy, Dr Mudie? We get a lot of them here. What a shame my husband is absent.'

'I recall your son defying the authorities. An heroic stand, it caused quite a stir.'

'A stir was caused here as well.'

'I was not of that calibre. I was meek and took what they handed out. Do you remember, Jaraby, a boy in our time who went on hunger strike?'

'No.'

'You must do. He refused to eat for four days. As a result, his breath became rather nasty. I think he has since died.'

'A boy? And Mr Turtle's death in public. The place is a slaughterhouse.'

'The boy died later, long after he had left the School. Perhaps in the war, I do not know. His name was curious: Bludgeon.'

'We do not talk much about the School unless my husband is here. He returns to those days. They were his most successful.'

'I go occasionally to an Old Boys' Day: many Old Boys are my patients. And personal recommendation counts for a lot.'

'Are you a Harley Street man, Dr Mudie?'

'Well, yes, I am.'

'I thought so. You have the air of the fashionable doctor. Basil had ideas of becoming a doctor once, but he is happier, I think, as he is.'

'What does he – what do you do, Jaraby?'

'I breed birds. Budgerigars.'

'They are beautiful creatures,' said Mrs Jaraby. 'Tame and talkative. Basil teaches them cheerful things to say.'

'They certainly are very popular at the moment. The sale of bird-seed has shot up since the war.'

'Did you hear that, Basil? The sale of bird-seed . . . That is a good omen from the business point of view.'

'As a child I had a parrot. We called it Jackie, I remember. It used to say "Abide with me, abide with me." We found it dead one day, in one of my father's fishing boots.' Dr Mudie, though well versed in the craft of small talk, placed a certain value on his time. He might continue this light conversation all night, but he saw no point in it. There was no sign of a prospective patient, no sign even of the man who had brought him this great distance on his one free afternoon.

'Would you care to see Basil's birds? They are suffering from a parrot's disease. You might well diagnose the trouble where veterinary experts have failed.'

'That is very kind of you, Mrs Jaraby. I fear I have no knowledge of bird diseases, and have always in fact been allergic to budgerigars. There is something about blue feathers that makes me a little uneasy.'

'How very odd. My husband kept a pet, an outsize cat, to which I was allergic.'

'Ah yes, a cat.'

'A cat is not a complete description. My husband purchased the animal from a man at the door many years ago, attracted I believe by the bargain price. The man passed on no pedigree, but the cat when it grew stood a couple of feet from the ground.'

'How very extraordinary.'

'What, what?' said Mr Jaraby, coming into the room.

'The Doctor is here and has been interesting us for an hour! You left him in the lurch, saying to come and then forgetting.'

'I never forgot. Mudie, my good man. I slipped to the post

office for a book of stamps and was delayed. I hope you have not been bored?'

'Not at all. No, no, I have been handsomely entertained.'

'Blackberry jelly sandwiches,' cried Mrs Jaraby. 'The larder could muster no more. Housekeeping on a shoestring, Dr Mudie.'

'A cup of tea, a cup of tea is what I crave.' Mr Jaraby sat down, annoyed.

'Basil has been talking of his birds. The sale of bird-seed has increased in leaps and bounds since the war. Ask Dr Mudie. Isn't that a good thing for us all, now that we have a business stake in the cultivation of feathered pets?'

'I do apologize,' said Mr Jaraby, 'for not being at home when you arrived. I trust you will not take it amiss. The Association keeps me busy with a heavy mail to see to.'

'The postmen complain,' remarked Mrs Jaraby. 'They come in vans with laden sacks. We think that soon they'll be charging a fee.'

'My wife cannot be serious. But you will understand how it is.'

'Of course,' said Dr Mudie, confused.

'He has been telling us of his parrot who sang a hymn, and how he fears blue feathers.'

'We have blue feathers here, Mudie. You would scarce believe the changes I came across on my return from Old Boys' Day. My cat was dead, a host of birds swarmed in and out of the rooms.'

'I am sorry about your cat, Mr Jaraby.'

'Were the cat alive today,' said Mrs Jaraby, 'you would not still be here. People did not stay long when Monmouth was at large. He had a finger off a gardener once.'

'The gardener struck or tantalized him.' Mr Jaraby set the record straight. 'He did not mind his finger gone. He told me so. He worked on afterwards, for several years.'

'Until another finger went.'

'That is not true. He lost one finger, that was all. You are trying to engage Dr Mudie's sympathies.'

'Dr Mudie, am I engaging your sympathies? Are you interested in the gardener or my husband's cat? You must forgive this domestic passage: the cat stays on to haunt the house, close to my husband's heart. Conversation is impossible without the cat.'

'Monmouth died in suspicious circumstances, Mudie. He was consigned to a dustbin by my wife. Would facts like that not play on your mind?'

'If little else is left to play,' answered Mrs Jaraby. 'Tell me, Dr Mudie, do you happen to know if the boys at that school are carrying on a chain letter that was started by a Major Dunkers of the Boer War?'

'Take no notice, Mudie,' Mr Jaraby said, chewing a sandwich.

'I'm afraid I have no information on that, Mrs Jaraby.'

'What a shame. I requested my husband to ascertain if it was so but, as he says, he took no notice.'

'Do you have some interest in the matter, Mrs Jaraby?'

'No, no,' Mr Jaraby interposed.

'In fact, yes, I have some interest. An old man who came here remembered the letter at that school sixty years ago. It thrived still when Basil was a boy. Perhaps you recall it yourself?'

'No, I fear I don't.'

'The School was cleared of those letters in my time,' said Mr Jaraby, 'I myself was instrumental in putting paid to the practice.'

'My husband's Housemaster, a queer man called Dowse, bade him do so, insisting that the letters had to do with pawnbrokers. I am anxious to know if the Major still survives.'

'Yes, it would be interesting. I imagine the point could be easily established. Did you ask amongst the boys, Mr Jaraby?'

'Good God, no!'

When Dr Mudie left, Mr Jaraby walked with him from the house to the bus-stop, saying on the way: 'Tell me what is in your mind. Tell me what you think, Mudie. Do not spare me, I can take the worst.'

'What do you mean, Mr Jaraby?'

'My wife. You heard her speak. How is the verdict? Do I not have your cooperation?'

'I don't quite follow.'

'Why not?'

'When last we met, Mr Jaraby, you talked about your wife. You feared for her, were nervous, felt for her condition. I confess I observed today no trace of the trouble you referred to.'

'You are telling me my wife is as sane as you or I?'

'One cannot speak of sanity or insanity so easily. From what I saw, Mrs Jaraby has all her wits about her. More wits than most at that age.'

'Are you deaf, Doctor? Did you not hear the extraordinary way she spoke of my cat? And gave you those sodden sandwiches?'

'But we must not –'

'No "but" at all. Did you fail to observe my son, that hair, those boots? He has not shaved since he came to the house.'

'But that is your son. We are speaking of your wife.'

'Her doing. She thinks nothing of his unshaven jowl, she encourages him in his ways. He was dyeing a bird yellow and dyed his hair as well. She bought the stuff for him; he will not stir outside. I tell you, I came into the room one day and found this fair-haired party hunched on the couch. "Good afternoon, sir," I said. "Are you a friend of Basil's?" He looked at me as though I were the one to be certified. Now that was not a pleasant thing to happen: my own son, his hair coloured like a woman's, staring at me like that.'

'I do not know what to say.'

'I imagined you would come with a form ready to fill in, and that that would be that. We would get her a bed somewhere, with others of her kind. My son would be given his marching orders and the house would settle down again.'

Mr Jaraby's father, an uncommunicative man, had had a way of examining his son rather closely and saying that he supposed blood was thicker than water. He had said little else to his son, but for all his life Mr Jaraby recalled the delivery of the words and the expression that accompanied them. That his father had disliked him was something he had come to accept as a child and for ever after; that in turn he disliked his own son was something he denied. 'For the right reasons,' Mr Jaraby held, 'I am prepared to like anyone on earth.' He added no proviso, for the proviso lay in the choice of words: *I am prepared* . . . He disapproved of his son, and when Basil put aside his habits and his ways he was prepared to begin the process of liking him. But when he considered him as he now was he could not even suppose, with his father, that blood was thicker than water. He saw no link with Basil, saw no repetition of himself; until there was an improvement in his son he would not see that even physically they had much in common.

Incorrectly, Dr Mudie thought that the return to the house had caused Basil to dye his hair: because his father was dark, because the two heads were similar in shape and the hair grew in a similar way, because Basil wished to differentiate himself as much as possible.

Dr Mudie said: 'Your son is a fully grown man. We cannot assume that his mother is responsible for all he does.'

'She says so, and asks me to take responsibility too.'

'If you don't mind my saying it, the situation is one you have to sort out yourself. Or between the three of you.'

'What does that mean? She will not listen to reason. Under her influence, neither will the boy.'

'He is no longer a boy.'

'I know, I know. The word slipped out. You are picking me up.'

'I'm sorry for that. I was trying to be a help.'

'You are hardly being that. You do not do what is required of you. We know what must be done in that house. It is painful, but I am made to bear it. See reason, Mudie.'

'Ask your doctor to give Mrs Jaraby a check-up. Explain to him your fears. He will soon evaporate them, and you can start with a clean slate. That is all I can say.'

'My doctor is a raving fool. He doesn't understand a word I say. He never listens.'

'But, Mr Jaraby, you must not have a raving fool as a doctor. Change, go to someone else.'

Frustration again faced Mr Jaraby. He had told his wife that in his public life all was well. It was true. In shops or on the street, in trains and buses he felt as always. He felt in command, able to insist on the course he chose to walk along a crowded thorough-fare, able to check the change he was handed, to demand and receive the goods he preferred. His wishes were observed; his word was law. So, within the month, should it be on the commit-tee. But what of Crimea Road? What of the house he owned and called his own? Must he accept that it was now an unreliable place, where anything could happen? The sitting-room and the garden, once havens of rest, were fearful places now; uneasy places, rich in defiance and chaos. He felt like furniture in the house, unnoticed by his son, played upon by his wife. He could no longer order the child his son had once been to obey him; he could not expect his will to be interpreted and acted upon. Had the change been gradual or had his will been stolen overnight? Mr Jaraby did not know. He could not see the picture clearly. The edges were blurred, the details haphazard. The mad and the wicked were in charge of his life in that house. They were tri-umphant, they mocked him.

Still, Mr Jaraby did not feel beaten. Other people had trouble-some families: intractable wives, unprepossessing sons. Mr Jaraby would go on his way with dignity, relying on the outside world to give him strength. He would stand out, a martyr if need be, against the forces that attempted to destroy him. For he knew he could not be destroyed. It troubled him only that men like Dr Mudie and Dr Wiley, men from the world outside, men from his public life, betrayed him in his need. And then – perhaps for no reason at all, or perhaps because his line of thought continued – he remembered the woman who had pursued him from Woolworth's to the teashop. For a moment he felt afraid, but in a minute the fear passed. There was some explanation for the woman. It could not be that the house spread its influence beyond its true domain. It could not be that he was no longer safe outside it. 'I shall hold my head high,' Mr Jaraby said to himself; and Dr Mudie, overhearing the statement, raised his eyebrows.

20

The idea that was running through Swingler's mind was that both Mr Jaraby and Mr Nox interested him. Mr Nox had telephoned and been rude. He had said he did not wish Swingler to continue his surveillance of Mr Jaraby; he said it was no longer important, that he did not wish to give Swingler another Italian lesson even if Swingler paid; that in fact, to speak bluntly, he disliked the kind of man that Swingler was. In reply Swingler was polite and curious. Mr Nox had told him very little; most of the time he had spoken in riddles. Swingler did not know why, precisely, he had been asked to keep an eye on Mr Jaraby; he did not know why Mr Nox wished to place him in disrepute. Swingler, who was never above suspecting the worst, suspected it now: Nox wished to 'have something' on Jaraby in order to extract money from him. Swingler, who had often himself 'had something' on people for that very reason, saw that the situation was bristling with possibilities. From what Nox had told him about Jaraby he was persuaded that if Jaraby had guilt it was worth something. If Nox could extract money, why not Swingler? Nox had all the signs of an amateur; Swingler was an expert. From what he had seen of Jaraby, the man was in something of a state. He had seen him emerge from a doctor's house and strike the brass plate with his stick. Now there was an odd thing to do. He had seen him fidget and lose composure when he sat in the Cadena with Angie. Yet Nox had said he was well used to such women. Jaraby was nervous and jumpy, and he looked as though he didn't like being like that. Maybe Nox had already made the discovery he was after, on his own. If that was so, Swingler didn't like it. 'Share and share alike' was Swingler's motto, though occasionally he deviated from it.

Then there was Nox himself. Nox was behaving very oddly. Nox, as Swingler saw it, was up to little good, however you looked at it. Could it be that Jaraby had something on Nox and that Nox wanted something on Jaraby to balance it? In that case, there was something to be had on Nox as well.

It was pleasant weather for watching people, and Swingler had nothing else to do. It was difficult for him to keep an eye on Nox because Nox knew who he was, but there was nothing to be lost by continuing his observation of Nox's enemy. He stepped out from behind a parked car in Crimea Road and followed Mr Jaraby to Mr Turtle's funeral. He trailed far behind him, dawdling and humming to himself. He always relied on his intuition: drama, Swingler felt, would sooner or later break through.

Drama of a kind had, in fact, broken through that same morning at the Rimini; and when later they attended their friend's funeral Mr Cridley and Mr Sole were the victims of shock, and still suffered considerable surprise.

'Fruit jelly,' Mr Cridley said at breakfast. 'It was marked fruit jelly on the menu. Fruit, I ask you. Did you have it, Sole? It was turnip in that jelly. I was up all night.'

'I made for the rice. Fruit jelly and fresh cream, it always says. And along it comes with custard. Rice is rice. A square chunk, cut from the dish.'

But it was not all this that worried them: they were well used to the shock of being served with custard when expecting cream, and of coming across orange-coloured lumps, beyond identification, in the jelly.

'Sole, look at what has just entered.'

Miss Burdock stood at the door, differently dressed. It was, apparently, that one day of the year: she wore already, at half-past eight in the morning, the flowered dress.

'Almighty God, attired like that for Turtle's funeral!'

Miss Burdock took her place at her own small table, requesting of the maid, as she always did, fruit juice and cornflakes, tea and brown toast. The two men gossiped, glancing at her.

'Lily.' Mr Sole called the maid. 'Lily, did Major Torrill leave a black tie behind?'

'I cannot believe,' exclaimed Mr Cridley, 'that she intends to attend the funeral in that get-up. One day in the year the woman goes gay, and it's for a funeral.'

'I didn't sleep a wink. Miss Edge in the corridor, someone flushing the lavatory, Turtle on my mind. I was in the sanatorium with him for a fortnight. He knew the name of every flower in the British Isles. In those days he had a phenomenal memory.'

'Who inherits?'

'Indeed. Not Burdock, please God. He spoke of his godson, Topham's boy. And a niece in Wales.'

'Is this it?' Lily asked, handing Mr Sole a black tie. 'There are hundreds there, striped and coloured. This was all there was in black.'

'A dressy fellow, Torrill. Lovely. Thank you, Lily dear.'

'Are we all set then?' Mr Cridley queried. 'Is there a collection at these affairs? Was there at your wife's? I was too upset to remember.'

'Good morning, gentlemen,' cried Miss Burdock, pausing at their table. 'Where are you off to, so smart you look?'

'We are attending,' answered Mr Sole stiffly, 'our friend Turtle's burial. No doubt we shall have the pleasure of your company in the church?'

'My company? Dear me, I am not dressed for so solemn an occasion. I don't feel a call to go; funerals are for families and old friends.'

'Are you saying you are not going to his funeral?'

'I could hardly intrude myself. After all, I scarcely knew Mr Turtle.'

'Scarcely knew him? Do you call being about to marry the man scarcely knowing him?'

'Who was about to marry him? Surely Mr Turtle was not arranging to marry again?'

'But Miss Burdock, you and Turtle were to marry. We all know about it. Turtle did not keep it a secret.'

'Did Mr Turtle say that? That he and I . . . ? Oh, Mr Sole! How sweet of Mr Turtle to wish for that. How very sweet!'

'He proposed, you accepted. That was what he said.'

'You dear old people, what fantasies you weave! Mr Turtle and I only went to the pictures and had tea. I hoped he would come to the Rimini as a resident; his big house was far beyond him. Oh, it has made my day to think that kind Mr Turtle had longed to marry me. How good of you to tell me!'

'I don't know about longed,' murmured Mr Cridley. 'Perhaps he thought you were the good housekeeping kind.' But Miss Burdock, her head turned, had gone on to her cubby-hole, where she would think about the news and might even have a weep.

'She led him on. She wanted to get him here. I call it diabolical.'

Mr Sole nodded.

'Motives, motives,' cried Mr Cridley, banging the breakfast table. 'You find them everywhere. Think of the awful Harp. How I hate these smart middle-aged people.'

A week ago, when Mr Turtle was alive, they would have rejoiced to hear that in his confusion he had mistaken the situation. Now they felt a little peeved that Miss Burdock had got off so lightly and was so pleased at the discovery of what had lurked in Mr Turtle's imagination before his death. Had they not spoken, she would never have known. Grumpily they set off for the sun-lounge and the morning mail.

All those people standing around in the heat by an open grave, they gave Swingler the willies. He was nervous because Mr Nox was there; he kept his hat pulled down over his forehead and his hand over his mouth.

The coffin lowered into a pit, earth falling on it: it seemed archaic and, to Swingler, something of a savage rite. Cremation, he considered, was the tidier end. Brass on the coffin gleamed, the clergyman's surplice was bright in the sunlight, the dry clay was caked and hardened into lumps.

Swingler saw Mr Nox standing alone, and Mr Jaraby with his big stick staring at him, as though about to set upon him. There was distrust and suspicion in the way Mr Jaraby was looking, and Swingler could see that Mr Nox was aware of it.

'Vouchsafe, we beseech Thee,' said the clergyman, 'to bless and hallow this grave, that it may be a peaceful resting-place for the body of Thy servant . . .'

Swingler saw two similar men who stood together, murmuring. 'I think she should have come anyway,' said Mr Cridley, 'and shown some respect.'

His friend agreed in hushed, though violent, tones. 'Burdock has no respect for a creature on earth, let alone one just removed from it.'

Mrs Strap was not at the funeral either. She was in Oxford Street buying lilac-coloured underclothes and twelve-denier stockings.

Basil was writing to A. J. Hohenberg . . . *psittacosis seems to be spreading. I have tried the tetracycline treatment you suggest but so far without avail. I would be glad of any further advice you can offer . . .* Basil and Mr Hohenberg had never met, but their correspondence, maintained now for close on five years, was a source of considerable comfort to him.

Swingler, chewing a match, followed Mr Jaraby back to Crimea Road.

21

It was too warm to sleep. Far too warm, Mr Jaraby thought, moving his body about the bed. Absurd to be so warm in London in July: had he not in his time known real heat in Burma? Was he not by this time a judge of what was right for London in July? Did anyone think he did not know that it was not some ersatz commodity, arbitrarily or even deliberately created by the fumes of heavy traffic and the increasing ubiquity of those electric signs? He sneered at the city, seeing the huge flashing neons and the new buildings and grown men eating chocolate on the pavements. The sheet beneath him felt like a rope; his pyjamas were damp and uncomfortable. He rose, switched on the light and remade his bed.

He lay on his back. If he chanced to drop off to sleep in this position he would, he knew, have a nightmare. But it was easier to relax like this, and Mr Jaraby had a theory that just at the moment of sleep he could turn gently on his side without upsetting his carefully coaxed drowsiness. He had held that theory for many years without ever succeeding in executing it. He lay still; first with his eyes closed and then with them open. It wasn't the heat at all, he thought: it was this damned business. God knows, it probably wasn't any warmer than any other night. God knows, probably the sweat on his body was the sweat of worry. Once you started worrying you couldn't stop. He accepted that he must put up with the condition of his wife; he was quite clear in his mind that she would continue to speak in her own particular way, and could no longer be relied upon to give him his due. At least the situation was as bad as it could become: nothing could be worse than Basil dropping cigarette ash all over the place and the chirruping of those birds. He would have a word or two with Basil and explain that it would be happier for all concerned if he thought about moving on; he would speak with subtlety and discretion. It was useless to consult doctors. The doctor of today couldn't see what was under his nose. Anyway, Mr Jaraby had other things to think about. He resented having worried about his wife, because that worry had led directly to this one. You start with one worry, you settle it in your mind; and then there's another. There was only a week to go before the committee meeting and he felt unprepared. He felt that he had not made sufficiently certain that nothing could go wrong. There was that extraordinary slander of Sanctuary's on Old Boys' Day. If Sanctuary was capable of such a ridiculous idea about Dowse, he was capable of anything: it didn't exactly give you confidence in the man's judgement. And Ponders was so weak, so likely to be swayed, and Nox was a trouble-maker. He went on thinking about them, seeing their faces, seeing their hands. Who would they have if they didn't choose him? Who would they have if there was a single real objection to his election? Not Cridley, not Sole; both were beyond it. Nor Nox, who was unpopular. Sanctuary? Sanctuary wouldn't be interested, though. Would they break the rule, which they were at liberty to break, and invite the new committee to choose its own President? Only once before had that been done, but it could be done and might be done. And if someone was fool enough to suggest Nox and Nox agreed, there was nothing he could do to prevent it; he could offer no real objection, no reason that was sound enough to be damaging.

An hour later a fresh thought struck Mr Jaraby and he rose again from his bed. His dressing-gown was twenty-three years old and had all the appearance of a well-worn garment. It served its purpose, though, and Mr Jaraby saw no sense in another purchase. That it was ragged and inadequate was a private affair, and inadequacy, he argued, was a question of degree. In the kitchen Mr Jaraby rooted in the waste-bin. There were potato peelings, a sodden paper-bag, tea-leaves, a soup tin and a tin that had contained peaches. It was this last that interested him. At supper he had noted the peaches, reminding himself that as soon as they were consumed he must question their origin with his wife. He had forgotten. Concerned with this other business, the thought had passed easily from his mind. He looked at the label and picked a tea-leaf from it. No need to question their origin now. *Cling peaches in rich syrup. Fourteen ounces. Australian.*

'My God,' said Mr Jaraby aloud.

The clock on the dresser ticked loudly. As he prepared to wake his wife he noticed with satisfaction that it registered twenty-five minutes past two.

'Come on now,' Mr Jaraby demanded in her bedroom. 'Cast sleep aside, we have a matter to discuss.'

Mrs Jaraby lay curled on her side, a white hair-net covering her head. He twisted the bedside lamp so that its beam fell on her face, an aid to her waking. She opened both eyes at once, and, seeing him there, immediately sat up. She said, as people often do in the confusion of being snatched from deep sleep: 'What is the time?'

'The time is irrelevant. Do not side-track me. I have not risen from my bed to discuss the time.'

'What then? Why do you wake me?'

'What of those peaches? Whence came our suppertime peaches? Tell me the truth, do not prevaricate.'

'Peaches?'

'Was other fruit mentioned? Did we enjoy some medley of fruit at supper? Do I enquire of cherries and pears and pine-apple?'

'Basil likes peaches. He has done so all his life.'

'You are avoiding my question. Cannot you be honest with a straight reply?'

'I do not understand you. I do not know why you are here, waking me and talking of peaches. Did the peaches injure you? Do you feel unwell?'

'The peaches were Australian peaches. They are clearly marked as such on the tin. Did you ascertain as you bought them that that was not so? That the label lies? I hope you did. I hope you have an explanation. At this late hour, I await it.'

'Good God above, are you mad? I bought the peaches in Lipton's. I have no idea –'

'You have no idea about anything. Tell me what *you* think you have no idea about, that I may set you straight.'

'I was going to say: I know nothing more about the peaches except that I bought them cheaply at Lipton's. The tin was damaged.'

'They were Australian peaches. They came from the Antipodes.'

'They could hardly be Australian and come from elsewhere.'

'I will not have Australian produce in the house.'

'So you say –'

'Then why go against my wishes? Why since you know them do you continue in your ways?'

'It is quite impossible to keep an eye on everything I buy. I have asked in the past about the butter and the bacon and the cheese. The people selling think me odd.'

'They think you odd for other reasons.'

'Maybe, maybe. I do not go into it with them. What is the time? I cannot help it if you dislike Australians and the place they come from. That is your own business, though what they have ever done to you I cannot imagine.'

'I dislike the way they speak. I will not have the house filled with Australian stuff. Cheap and nasty, as the people are. God knows, the house is bad enough. Must you make it worse?'

'It is your house, of your choice. You are making me answerable for everything.'

'You are answerable for the depths to which we have sunk. Peaches in tins, birds and cigarette ash.'

'I shall not sleep again, woken at this hour.'

'I have not slept at all. My eyes haven't closed.'

'So you share your sleeplessness with me. Wake Basil too, and make all three of us a pot of coffee.'

'There is no need to wake Basil. There is no need for coffee. I have spoken to you of the matter in hand, and I shall bid you goodnight.'

'You seem to be out of your senses. You are in senility. Shall I tell Dr Wiley that you woke me at this hour and talked ravingly about peaches? What would his rejoinder be? That we must attend directly to having you certified and put out of harm's way?'

'It is you, not I, who need all that.'

'No, no. I do not walk through the rooms at night chanting about a tin of peaches. Do you think the Australians are planning an invasion of this country and send us poisoned food? Is that what goes on in your tortured mind? Paranoia seems well to the fore.'

Mr Jaraby left the room.

At breakfast Mr Jaraby said: 'What do you make of this business? I cannot recall your having offered an opinion.'

Mrs Jaraby, in a dressing-gown and still wearing her white hair-net, poured tea from a flowered pot. She preferred to dress at a later hour, since it was a rule of her husband's that they sit down to breakfast at fifteen minutes past six. 'What is it?' she enquired vaguely. 'What are you talking about?'

Mr Jaraby sighed. 'I am talking about the worry that has kept me awake all night.'

'The peaches?'

'Why on earth should they keep a man awake at night? I assure you I have more to think about than some stupidity over tinned fruit.'

'I am racking my brain to find a reason for your sleeplessness.'

'Why should you do that? If you ask I will answer you.'

Mrs Jaraby smeared marmalade on toast. 'Then I ask, I ask.'

'Do you know that in the night I counted up the amount I have spent on business for the Association during the last two years? Twenty-six pounds. That is a rough approximation: it may be far more. Add the cost of writing-paper and envelopes, blotting paper, ink, time and energy that might have been turned to some financial endeavour. Shall I tell you what this amounts to? A lesson in ingratitude.'

'What is a lesson in ingratitude? I don't follow.'

'One to another they say: Jaraby's work is done, Jaraby has had his position on the committee, now he goes to grass. That's what they say: Jaraby's work is complete.'

'And is it complete? If you have spent all that money on stamps, you must have achieved something.'

'It is not complete. I have other plans. Changes, reorganization. As President I would have implemented all that was in my mind.'

'Then what can the trouble be? Are you not to be President any day now? And will it mean that you will have to spend so much money?'

'I am eaten by doubt. I tell you that man-to-man. I fear that my election will not be automatic. Sanctuary seems unbalanced; Nox is a black trouble-maker.'

'Do you know, that has never been apparent from your conversation.'

'What has not?'

'What you say: that Mr Nox is an African.'

'An African? He is not an African. I did not say so. Of course he isn't. He's just a damned busybody. Ponders, Sole, Sanctuary, Boyns, Cridley, Turtle – putty in his hands.'

'Well, certainly you have said that the last named is dead. And buried with appropriate ceremony.'

'You are thoughtlessly irritating with these remarks. Have I not enough to think about without your attempting to make it worse?'

'This hour for breakfast is no longer a satisfactory arrangement. Our nerves are frayed, our tempers imposed upon. Now that Basil is back, shall we make it nine o'clock? He does not rise as early as this, and as it is I am obliged to prepare breakfast twice.'

'He must fit in with us, not we with him. This has always been our hour.'

'Not mine; it is an imposition for me to rise like this. You no longer leave the house in the mornings; this is a needless relic of earlier days. It is an arbitrary time in our present life.'

'It suits me to keep the habit up. It is not a bad one. What have you against it?'

'Nothing, so long as I do not feature in it myself. As I shall not from tomorrow on. Breakfast at nine for three.'

'So you deny me breakfast! You cannot buy things properly, and now you deny me my simple needs.'

'If the housekeeping displeases you make fresh arrangements; or see to what irks you yourself.'

'I cannot go on with these petty things. I was talking about the committee. Why did you side-track me? A unanimous confirmation, a vote of confidence, is that too much to ask? After every effort on my part, sleepless nights, train fares, speech-making, organizing?'

'And the money on stamps. You must ask for it back if they do not make you President.'

'I remember Nox. I remember Nox, he used to be my fag. Mark it well, that man wiped my boots daily for two whole years. And bloody badly he did them. A hairy-faced boy. D'you know, he nearly *died* on the cricket field? Struck by a cricket ball on the forehead, down like a ninepin. Lump the size of a mango, and off came our caps. Thinking, you see, we were in the presence of death. And there he is now, terrible little man. Every time I see him I think: kick in the pants, bloody great kick in the pants.'

Mr Jaraby's fingers drummed angrily on the table. He watched his wife dropping off to sleep. He ceased to play with his fingers, waiting for her head to droop; when it did, as her chin sank down on her chest, his voice began again:

'I shall telephone Nox this morning. I shall speak to the man in an effort to clear the air and see what is in his mind. I cannot accept that, fool though he may be, he does not see that we of the same generation must stick together. You understand what I am talking about? You are not asleep, are you?' He paused and continued: 'The committee would be unanimous but for Nox. I'm sure of it. Do you understand?'

'Yes, yes. Nox is the nigger in the woodpile.' She had been dreaming when he woke her up in the night. She dreamed she was a child again and ran around in an Alice in Wonderland dress.

'There was some trouble with Nox's bladder,' Mr Jaraby said, smiling a little. 'I recall distinctly a red rubber mat on which he slept.'

'I imagine all that is behind him now.'

'Do you? And why should it be? The fellow is diseased, his difficulty may well be a symptom.' He laughed, and was angered that she did not join in with him.

Mrs Jaraby rose and collected the breakfast things on a tray. Her practice was to carry crockery and cutlery to the kitchen, tidy up generally, and return to bed.

'Yes, I shall ring Nox this morning. In fact, suit the deed to the hour, I shall do it now.'

'It is twenty-five past six.'

'It is. He will hardly have left the house on some errand, if that is what you are suggesting.'

'No, no. Merely that he may not be up yet.'

'Are you so well in tune with the good Nox's habits then? Ha, ha, is there something between you and this elderly ragamuffin?'

'Oh, really –'

'Why do you wear that awful hair-net?'

But his wife had passed from the room, and, though hearing the question, saw no point in replying.

'Look here, Nox, you can probably guess why I am telephoning.'

There was a silence. Then a voice said: 'Who is that?'

'Jaraby, Nox. Jaraby here.'

Again there was a moment of silence, before Nox said: 'Is something wrong?'

'My good Nox, you are the better judge of that.'

'I'm sorry, Jaraby. I would rather you came to the point. Do you know what time it is?'

'Certainly, my dear fellow: it is precisely six-thirty.'

'You woke me up.'

'Look here, Nox, we must settle this matter of next session's President once and for all.'

'At this time of the morning? I do not sleep easily, Jaraby. I do not take kindly to this.'

My God, Mr Jaraby thought, the swine has cut me off.

Slowly, as meticulously as if engaged upon a surgical incision, Mr Nox opened his mail. He read the letters with equal industry, thus avoiding a bothersome return to the detail of their contents. There was little to interest him. He poured himself a cup of coffee and devoted his mind to the telephone call he had earlier received. It had resulted in his being obliged to lie in bed reading instead of continuing his sleep. How like Jaraby, he reflected, to impose such a discomfort on him. If the argument was that people do not change, he supposed that Jaraby was a good example of it. Jaraby today was much as Jaraby had been sixty years ago: a thoughtless fellow, crude in his ways. Jaraby had flung a boot at him and caused a bruise to rise on his forehead. From Jaraby's lips had issued all the conventional insults about his family and their possessions.

Mr Nox tried to put him from his mind. He prepared the room for the morning's lesson. But as he sharpened the pencils and laid out paper he saw himself vividly in retrospect, standing perfectly still, obeying the instruction, while Jaraby sat and stared at him.

Later that morning, at eleven forty-two, Basil Jaraby was arrested. Swingler, talking to a man who had just delivered coal to number fourteen, saw the black car draw up at number ten and watched the men walk heavily towards the front door. He paused in mid-sentence and drew the coalman's attention to the proceeding, saying that it looked like trouble.

On the Air Ministry roof it was eighty degrees Fahrenheit. In the London parks the attendants prepared for the lunchtime rush on deck-chairs. In offices in Mayfair and Holborn and the City men worked in shirt-sleeves, thinking of holidays and weekends. Mrs Strap, in her lilac underclothes and a pale dress, bought a sundae in the cafeteria at Bourne and Hollingsworth. At Lord's England were eight for no wicket.

In Crimea Road it was a quiet morning. A woman wheeled a shopping-basket on a handle. Another shelled peas in her back garden, a radio shrilling popular music beside her. 'Is it all right,' asked Basil in the police car, 'to light a cigarette?'

'Ah, Mr Swingler,' said the sergeant at the desk. 'Long time no see.'

'Long time velly busy,' said Swingler amusingly. 'How about this Jaraby fellow?'

22

'I have information that would interest you,' Swingler cooed into the telephone. 'Interest you very, very much.'

It would be in the papers. But before it got there, before Mr Nox knew anything about it, before Mr Nox knew that it was the kind of information he could read for free in time – before any of that came about, Swingler held a trump card.

'Our association is done with, Swingler. I made that clear.'

'Man dear, this is the goods. This is important. I'm telling you I have a first-class tip.'

'I am in the middle of a lesson. If you have something to say, say it.'

'I think, Mr Nox, you might find this worth something.'

'Worth something? Worth what?'

'Say fifty pounds?'

'Now look here, Swingler –'

'It doesn't matter to me, Mr Nox. You just take it or leave it. I can offer you more than you ever asked me to discover. This is the real McCoy, as we call it.'

'Come on then. Come on with it. Let me judge how real it is for myself.'

'Fifty?'

'Twenty, Swingler.'

'Sorry, Mr Nox, this is too good for less than fifty notes.'

'All right, all right. Come to the point, please.'

'Fifty in cash. Have fifty ready in cash. I shall be with you within the hour.'

'You must tell me first –'

'Ah, Mr Nox, that is not at all the usual procedure.'

'But I am buying a pig in a poke.'

'Precisely, Mr Nox. A first-class pig, a first-class poke! I am on my way to you. The winged Mercury makes haste to bear the tidings!'

Swingler smiled. He went to the bathroom and brushed his teeth. It was something he always did in a moment of triumph.

'It cannot affect me,' Mr Jaraby said to himself. 'The son was disowned. There is nothing about the sins of the children being visited on the fathers. I am innocent in all this. No one will mention it.'

'I shall mention it,' cried Mrs Jaraby. 'As often as you mention that frightful cat or Australian food.'

'Do you threaten me?'

'No. I put the sentence badly. What I should have said was: as often as you have mentioned those things in the past so often in the future shall I be given to mentioning the other thing.'

'I was not thinking of you, of what you shall be given to saying or doing. I was thinking of other people.'

'Other people will notice and note. In many minds you may be confused with your son, his action taken for yours. You may find that people fight shy of you, and do not care to have you about. Shopkeepers may serve you rapidly, other shoppers stand well away from you. Ours is not a usual name. One Jaraby is easily mistaken for another. It is the superficial thing, the name, that clings in people's minds. They learn of these things carelessly, not bothering to remember the details or the age and appearance of the wrong-doer. I saw the house being pointed out today. It was as if a murder had taken place. We have much to prepare for; you more than I. I bear the name, but I am a woman: my sex sees me through.'

'But I am entirely innocent. I have done nothing at all.'

'Be that as it may – and I am not saying that I confirm your plea – you shall reap a savage harvest. A little time elapses and seeing you abroad they shall cry: "Jaraby is no longer imprisoned. Jaraby has paid for his crime. There he goes, a free man: three cheers for British justice!" But they will remember to shun you, and tell their companions of the story that surrounds your name.'

'This is just wild talk again; nonsensical rambling.'

'No, it is true. "Wasn't there something disgraceful about that man?" they will try to recall. "Jaraby the name was, it was in the papers".'

'There is no need for it to be in the papers. It will be summarily and quietly dealt with; without publicity.'

'You would have liked Basil to have called himself Brown or Hodges, would you? When years ago you disowned him you would have wished him to hand you back your name? To go away from us and live a stranger with a *nom de guerre*?'

'It might have been the decent thing,' cried Mr Jaraby. 'It might have been the decent thing when he knew he displeased us, to go away and worry us no more, and take a name that cut off all connexion.'

'You must not say he displeased *us*. He did not ever displease me. I love my son. You never learnt to like him.'

'I was prepared to. Since he was a child on my knee I was prepared to.'

'Being prepared is a pretty watery thing. You had more regard for your cat. The cat would take what you gave him, and you did not know if he hated you or not.'

'Monmouth did not hate me.'

'Do not be too sure. You must not take the dumbness of a beast to mean whatever you wish it to mean.'

'Monmouth and I were friends. You cannot take that away.'

'Your relationship with your late cat is entirely your own affair. You speak of a cat, I of a son. Is there something to be learnt from that?'

'So in all your magnanimity you condone what has happened?'

'If you mean, do I condone the crime for which Basil has been arrested, the answer is no. I do not condone it; but he is not yet guilty of it.'

'The police would not have come had he been innocent. They

would not have picked him out of all the millions in the country. He has a bad record; we should have expected something like this.'

'His record, as you call it, is in his favour. It suggests a certain instability and may be a cause of leniency. But he is not on trial here. The law requires us to think of him as innocent.'

'He should not have come back to this house. I should have shown more intolerance. I would give my right hand to have been spared this.'

'Keep your hand; its use is limited when taken from the arm. We have not a monopoly of suffering in this affair. We are bystanders, as befits people of our age. Others bear the burden of the suffering.'

'You are at the root of it, inviting him back, enticing him and those birds to the room upstairs. We would not be concerned but for that.'

'How could we not be concerned since we are the parents? You cannot lock yourself in the past as you seek to do. The present is the only reality.'

'I do not lock myself in the past. I am concerned with the present, and the future too.'

'We will not muddle through an argument on that. We have time enough awaiting us. And this other thing takes precedence today.'

'It cannot affect me,' Mr Jaraby repeated. 'It is wrong and unjust that it should.'

'You have played a confidence trick on me,' Mr Nox said. 'The information is good, I grant you, but it would have come my way automatically.'

'You had it early, sir. You can act on it at once. It is valuable to be a jump ahead.'

'In this case it is of little value.'

'Was I to know that? Was I in possession of that fact?'

'No, Swingler, in truth you were not.'

'Well, I'll be saying cheerio then, Mr Nox.'

'There is just one thing, Swingler.'

'Sir?'

'When this gets into the papers it would be a help if all the personal details were correct. For instance, a mention of the school the man attended.'

'Yes, well –'

'It might interest the public. To say that a man has been to a certain public school sets the scene.'

'You are making sense, Mr Nox.'

'And you with your influence should be able to drop the facts into a couple of reporters' ears.'

Swingler laughed. 'Who better, Mr Nox? Who better than Thos Swingler?'

'Precisely.'

'Say another twenty-five?'

'Ten, Swingler. You have had fifty by means of sharp practice.'

'Settle for fifteen, Mr Nox. A round sixty-five and our business is concluded.'

'Is that Mr Jaraby?'

'Jaraby speaking.'

'You don't know me, but I have reason to believe that I can be of comfort and help to you. Could I trespass on five minutes of your time?'

'Who are you, sir?'

'Known as Swingler, Mr Jaraby. Thos Swingler, friend to the worried. I am sorry about your little domestic trouble. That recent happening in Crimea Road. Mr Jaraby will need help, I said to myself. So here I am, sir; my services at your disposal.'

'Are you a reporter?'

'Far from it, sir. But you ask a good question. I suggest, Mr Jaraby, that this is a matter in which our friends of the press may well go to the fair. Believe me, there's nothing they like better than playing up the public school angle.'

'I don't think the press will be interested.'

'There you are wrong, sir. The scribes of the press, Mr Jaraby, hard-faced men without soul, are at this very moment elbowing politics off the front pages. Like a swarm of wasps they are, congregating round a saucer of raspberry jam.'

'Why are you in touch with me?'

'Swingler, I said, hasten to that poor man's aid. Mr Jaraby, sir, I am in a position to prevent the worst. What would you say if I agreed to reduce the publicity to a minimum? The name misspelt, the address a previous one, all mention of educational academies removed?'

'How could you do that, Mr Swingler?'

'With money, sir. Say five hundred pounds, in cash. Shall we meet together in some quiet place? Tomorrow morning?'

23

Mr Nox telephoned Sir George Ponders.

'I shall oppose Jaraby as President at next week's meeting.'

'Oppose Jaraby? Why do that? Have you some grounds?'

'Something unpleasant that has come to light.'

'Some scandal, Nox?'

'Enough to make it wise to keep the Jaraby name beneath the bushel.'

'Speak plainly: what is it?'

'Jaraby's son has just been arrested on a serious charge.'

'His son – not Jaraby himself?'

'Not Jaraby himself.'

'But in that case –'

'In the interests of the School, Jaraby must not be President.'

Sir George Ponders telephoned General Sanctuary.

'Do you know about this, Sanctuary? Nox has been on to me about Jaraby's son.'

General Sanctuary sighed, thinking of his garden and his bees. He said: 'What's the matter with his son?'

'Nothing's the matter with him. The chap's done something.'

'Jaraby's a funny fellow.'

'It's his son Nox is on about.'

'Yes, well, what does he say about his son? I don't understand any of this.'

'Neither do I. Nox says he will oppose Jaraby as President.'

'Why should Nox say that?'

'Jaraby's son has been arrested.'

★

'They have arrested Basil Jaraby,' said Mr Cridley.

'Who have arrested Basil Jaraby?'

'Guess, Sole, guess.'

'Do you mean the police have taken the boy?'

'If Nox has got his facts right, they have handcuffed Jaraby minor and carried him away from Crimea Road.'

'He was not there when we visited them.'

'He is not there now. The parents wail and gnash their teeth.'

'Jaraby will take that hard.'

'His son may take it harder.'

'Did Nox give details? Why has it happened? Was Basil Jaraby drunk?'

'A serious charge, Nox said. A big court case to follow. He implied it would make a stir.'

'For goodness' sake, what mischief has the lad got himself into?'

'A grave offence, Nox said; no more.'

'You should have asked him. It would have been a natural question.'

'Nox says it will affect Jaraby going up as President.'

A week later Mr Jaraby telephoned Mr Swabey-Boyns.

'Jaraby here. Look here, this lunatic Nox is against my going up as President. What do you say, Boyns?'

'This is extraordinary,' Mr Swabey-Boyns said. 'Do I know you, sir? My name is Swabey-Boyns. I am relaxing just now. Who is that there?'

'Jaraby on the line. Nox is opposing me as President. He will speak on Friday.'

'Say your name clearly, Jaraby, and thus avoid confusion. Well, well, Nox has reasons no doubt. Let us hear them. Let us give the man the floor and hear him air his views. Funny. I was thinking only last night of the day you locked Haw minor in the lavatory.'

'This is a serious matter, Boyns. Nox is out to make –'

'It was a serious matter for Haw minor as I recall.'

'Be that as it may, it has nothing to do with what we are discussing.'

'You nailed the door on the outside. Or screwed it maybe. The poor devil was there for eighteen hours.'

'I don't remember that. Which lavatory was it?'

'The one at the back of Dowse's. Haw minor was inside – you, with carpenter's kit, without.'

'Oh, quite impossible. Certainly it wasn't me. You will be present on Friday, Boyns?'

'Yes, of course I shall. Incidentally, I must remind you that my name is Swabey-Boyns. I do not address you as Jar.'

'Dear fellow, a slip of the tongue. Have to watch Nox, you see. The madman is out to make trouble. Stand together against the upstarts, eh? Remember Nox on the cricket field?'

'Ha, ha, ha,' said Mr Swabey-Boyns, thinking of Haw minor in the lavatory.

'This says there is no need to let grey hair make you look older than your years, or to resort to dyes and rinses with their embarrassing change of colour. Nox says that was how they caught young Jaraby out. His hair was white and his beard black. I should have thought that was elementary.'

Mr Sole said: 'We should ring up old Boyns and remind him of the committee meeting.'

'I'm going to write to this one. I'm most interested in this.'

'Boyns can never be relied upon.'

'You see to him then, like a good fellow. I shall pen a letter.'

'Be careful now: that very advertisement may well have been young Jaraby's undoing. You can trust nothing you read. Remember Harp.'

'There is no harm in writing. I shall not commit myself.'

'Put S.A.G. on the back of the envelope. My mother used to do that, every letter she sent.'

'S.A.G. Whatever for?'

'St Anthony guide, it means.'

Mr Nox telephoned Mr Swabey-Boyns.

'Do not forget Friday's meeting. I shall oppose Jaraby as President. It will be an important occasion.'

'What's that?' asked Mr Swabey-Boyns.

'Can you hear me? The meeting on Friday: you will be there?'

'Of course I shall be there. I never miss a meeting. Who is that speaking?'

'Nox. Well, I look forward to seeing you.'

'My God,' said Mr Swabey-Boyns, returning to his jigsaw.

Mr Sole telephoned Mr Swabey-Boyns.

'Just to remind you about Friday, old man. Best bib and tucker, you know.'

'The meeting? Yes.'

'Dinner beforehand, don't forget.'

'I'm doing a jigsaw now. You are interrupting me.'

'Sorry about that. Don't forget, best bib –'

'Why are you assing about in that funny way? Are we a couple of infants? I can't stand here talking about bibs.'

'You may remember,' Mr Sole retorted sharply, 'that the last time you had to borrow Cridley's overcoat to cover yourself at the dinner-table. Having turned up in garments with paint on them.'

'What?' said Mr Swabey-Boyns.

'You had paint on your clothes.'

'I wish to God you people would stop telephoning me.'

Swingler made for the Italian Riviera. Sipping a glass of gin and lemon as he waited for his plane, he felt a sorry smile flit across his face. To think that the two old men had imagined that for such paltry sums one could tamper with the freedom of our

British press. The smile cheered up; no doubt about it, he still had an eye for a situation. His lips moved soundlessly, practising his Italian.

Mr Jaraby telephoned Mr Nox.

'Jaraby here. Look here, Nox, about this matter of the –'

'You are coming to the meeting?' Mr Nox asked. 'Well then, we can discuss the whole question there.'

24

Mr Swabey-Boyns was casting his mind back. He was drowsy; euphoria dominated him. He moved the brandy around in his glass, watching it and delighting in the moment. It was that good moment just after dinner, a moment of relative clarity for Mr Swabey-Boyns, before the feeling of intoxication descended on him. It invariably did descend after such a dinner, because Mr Swabey-Boyns was greedy about brandy.

They sat in evening dress, some with decorations pinned to their breast, seven men round a table. There was an extra chair and an extra place because originally, months before, the table had been ordered for eight. Mr Swabey-Boyns, sitting between Mr Sole and Mr Nox, recalled the moment when – known then as Boyns major – he had been marched from the examination hall, his arms and the palms of his hands rich in minute information to aid him with an algebra paper. There had been, then, the whole school assembled and the thrashing of Swabey-Boyns in view of all, as an example against his deed. 'Will you live that down, sir?' H. L. Dowse had cried. But he had. In some clever way he turned the incident to his advantage; adding thereby something to his prestige. When he shaved now in the mornings he saw a face that was shot with shredded veins; he saw hands that quivered as they scraped away the soap, eyes that were often not up to the task of assessing his handiwork. Once he had been Boyns major of great repute; arrogant and powerful; swaggering, magnificent Boyns; Boyns in some trouble over a boy called Slocombe, accused of corrupting the boy and lying his way to safety. He had run into Slocombe five or six years ago, just before his death: beetle-browed, moustached, his face scrawny, the flesh seeming of some other substance, Slocombe who had been in his time the beauty of the Lower Fourth, Slocombe whose hand he had clutched on a walk, to whom he had later read the *Idylls of the King*.

'Remember the day the old Queen came?' Sole was muttering excitedly beside him. 'The flags and the cheering?' Sole who had been sick in Chapel during the singing of hymn 13, causing the place to reek of whisky.

Mr Jaraby smiled round the table. The President was in the Chair.

'Shall I put my case, Ponders? Shall I put my case since already I have been put forward as your successor?'

'Order,' said Sir George vaguely. 'We know the case, I think. Let us be quick about this and hear of any objections. We are agreed that Jaraby takes my place next session?'

Mr Nox shook his head, rising to his feet. 'No, Mr Chairman, we are not entirely agreed. I do not agree. I am for reviewing the case.'

'Look here, Nox –' Mr Jaraby began.

'Order, eh?' Sir George suggested.

'Does Jaraby deny it?' said Mr Nox, his voice like steel upon steel. 'Does Jaraby deny that his son has posed as a major in the army for the purpose of gaining credit from holiday hotels? Does he deny that this son is now behind bars for a graver crime?'

The eyes of the men sought neutral corners to fix on; matches were struck and the brandy passed slowly again. Mr Jaraby, his hands gripping the sides of his chair, struggled to hold his anger.

'Does Jaraby deny that Basil Jaraby, his son, was arrested in disguise at twenty minutes to twelve on the morning of August the twenty-second?'

'Now, now,' Sir George murmured.

'Does Jaraby deny –'

'Nox is a Jew,' shouted Mr Jaraby.

Mr Nox appeared surprised. 'In fact I am not a Jew. I have never been. But were I of that race I would fail to see its relevance at this moment.'

'You're a stupid bloody fool,' Mr Jaraby shouted, his face very red, sweat gleaming on his forehead. He banged the table with his hand. 'Stupid, stupid –'

'Oh come now,' Sir George interceded. 'Really, this is no way to carry on. What has befallen Jaraby's son does not concern us, eh?'

'Jaraby's son is an Old Boy of the School. The newspapers remark on it. I think in the circumstances Jaraby should have the decency to stand down.'

'We must abide by the rules laid down,' Mr Nox said. 'I have stated an objection to this man as President. I have stated it in the interests of the School. It is an objection that stands up well to scrutiny. That is all that is required.'

'We must keep our heads,' Mr Cridley remarked.

'Jaraby has done good work for the Association,' said Mr Sole. 'That goes without saying. It seems a pity now –'

'I am being attacked on a personal count. Nox dislikes me and trumps up a case.'

Mr Nox shook his head. 'No. You have done nothing to be ashamed of. You have done nothing at all. It is just unfortunate, that is all. We are asking you to react as a gentleman.'

'I have my rights.'

'So has the School. Do you wish to insist upon rights that injure the School? Where does our duty lie on this committee?'

'I know my duty, Nox. My duty lies in my work; the work I have done for the Association, the work I may continue.'

'Publicity and confusion must be taken into consideration. You are rendered unsuitable and should accept it.'

'You are after the post yourself, Nox. You are playing politics. You turn a private issue into a public one. The School has little to be proud of in you.'

'Less to be proud of in your son.'

'He is not on trial here. It is not he who is called upon to fill the Presidency.'

Mr Nox laughed lightly, appealing to the rest of the committee.

'Jaraby will not see reason.'

'Let us see the facts objectively,' said Mr Cridley. 'We must be hasty in neither direction. What is there to consider? We must weigh the pros and cons.'

'Cridley, Cridley,' exclaimed Sir George with irritation. 'Surely you know what we are considering? Surely you know the pros and cons by now?'

'Read any newspaper,' put in Mr Nox.

'One cannot go by the newspapers. We must deliberate on the matter, sort out irrelevancies, consider how our decision will affect the welfare of the School.'

'We have heard all that,' Sir George said. 'We are trying to do as you say. Our efforts speak for themselves: we do not have to announce everything step by step.'

'I was merely drawing the threads together, Ponders, to allow us to examine what we have to examine with logic rather than emotion. Is there something wrong in that?'

'No, of course there isn't.'

'If Jaraby were of the same character as his son we would not hesitate to support Nox's objection. But that is not the case. That is very far from being the case. Yet, as Nox suggests, there is good reason to believe that publicity of this nature might well associate itself with the miscreant's father. There is unquestionably no doubt –'

'Cridley, have you taken too much to drink? You are rambling on like a sheep in a fog.'

Mr Cridley seemed taken aback. After a short pause he said:

'In that case I shall cease. One tries to throw a little light and receives insults for one's pains.'

'I remember once,' Mr Swabey-Boyns began, 'I was standing in Cloisters waiting for that little man – what's his name? Mitcham was it? – to give me an organ lesson –'

'Has this got to do with what we are discussing, Boyns?'

'No, no, this was in '03. I saw Mitcham coming towards me and I thought it might be quite an amusing thing to –'

'I'm sorry, Boyns, we must have order.'

'Are you forbidding me to continue?'

'Unless what you say is relevant.'

'In that case, Ponders, I must request you to give me the benefit of my full name. I do not address you as Pond.'

'It is unfair and unjust,' General Sanctuary said, 'that Jaraby should be made to suffer for his son. A doctor is not struck from practice because his son commits adultery. A soldier is not cashiered because his child steals. There is nothing in the rules of our Association that says we should now behave differently. We must act with due integrity; uncowed by the narrowness of other people's view. Shall we be seen to act unjustly to a man, to condemn without reason? Well? I see I am failing as I speak: I cannot sway you. You are lost and afraid and anxious. You fear that if Jaraby is elected tonight he will in time be asked to resign by the Headmaster and the Governors. They will argue that the breath of scandal must be kept from the School, that his name must not be a reminder to Old Boys and parents. You feel that the matter will be taken thus out of your hands, your decision reversed, and you yourselves held up to the ridicule of younger men as bumbling and incapable. You have no strength left with which to contradict. You do not care, but you cannot bear to see the underlining of your impotence. You pretend you act in wisdom, for the good of the majority. But you know you act in fear, for the good of nobody.'

General Sanctuary finished his brandy and rose to his feet.

'I am no part of this pettiness. I resign at once from this committee.'

'He is not my son,' cried Mr Jaraby. 'My wife's only. By a previous marriage.'

The men stared at their hands, embarrassed by the pathos in the lie.

25

Rain came on the night of the committee meeting. It dripped from the garden gnomes in Crimea Road and lay in pools on the caked lawns. The sky was dark and bleak; dried leaves rattled on the suburban trees. In small back gardens children's toys lay scattered, their tired paint revived. Wallflowers and the last of the roses were fresh again in the gloom.

The rain spread from the west. It fell in Somerset in late afternoon; it caught the evening crowds unprepared in London. A woman, glad to see it, walked through it in a summer dress. A man in Putney, airing his dog, lost his dog on the common and died in October of a cold that had become pneumonia. The umbrellas of the cautious, a handful only, moved smugly through Knightsbridge. Seagulls darted on the river; elderly tramps huddled around a tea-stall near Waterloo Bridge, talking of winter doss-houses. Women whose place was the streets stared at the rain morosely from windows in Soho, wondering how the change would affect their business and guessing the worst. People with rheumatism said it would affect their bones and recalled the pain that the damp air presaged.

At the Rimini the water leaked through a cracked pane in the sun-lounge, dripping dismally on to a hat of Mr Sole's. Miss Burdock picked garden tools from the paths and flower beds: secateurs and clippers, various trowels and forks. With an old cape of Major Torrill's thrown over her head, she returned them to their rightful place in the summer-house, whispering about the carelessness of several residents, naming them in her mind. She would speak to them tomorrow: if they wished to potter in her garden they must prove their worth. There was malicious damage in the wallflower beds; and Miss Edge had cropped the daisy chrysanthemums. Not even the rain would save them now.

In a public-house in Barking Mrs Strap sat in one bar and Mr Harp in another. They did not know one another, nor did they know that men he had once met had been lifelong friends of the man whose money now bought her a row of whiskies. It was not even a coincidence that they were there; it was not even extraordinary. And though they met before the night was out and walked together through the rain, they did not discover that there was a conversation they might have had.

Mr Jaraby walked slowly along Crimea Road. The rain soaked his trousers and was cold on his skin. He walked beneath the orange glow of electric light, trailing his stick a bit, moisture in the crevices of his face. He tried to count how many days it had been since it rained before. He talked to himself, counting and reminiscing. A dog came towards him and he recognized it as the one that had been Monmouth's enemy. Its owners complained that Monmouth had torn half its tongue out. 'A fair fight,' he had retorted, closing the door on a woman in an overall. 'I saw it myself,' he told her husband. 'The dog began it.' The dog was a big Kerry Blue, a rare enough breed these days. It skulked along the pavement, well away from him, smelling the ground. Its owners said it had been valuable but was no longer so, with only the roots of a tongue left. Mr Jaraby watched its damp, dark haunches shift through the rain. He made the clicking noise one makes to attract a dog's attention. It was too far away to hear.

In the house he took his clothes off and replaced them with pyjamas striped grey and green. He put on his dressing-gown and lay on his bed listening to the rain.

Watching the play, Mrs Jaraby could hear the rain on the french windows. On the small screen a blonde woman in a white jumper was talking to a youth in a tweed overcoat in a kitchen. The youth moved from the kitchen to a sitting-room, stripping off his overcoat. The woman had a face like a cat's, though prettier than

Monmouth's. She entered the sitting-room with a tray, and something that might have been an altercation took place over a gramophone record. The youth put on his overcoat again and began to leave; he changed his mind, taking off the overcoat. The two embraced, the woman stroking the youth's hair.

Then the woman was pulling the curtains back, and Mrs Jaraby guessed it must be morning; although she was puzzled by the macintosh that the woman was wearing. The youth was still in bed, playing with a pillow, speaking angrily.

Suddenly, in the same flat, there was a man in shirt-sleeves and waistcoat, washing his hands in the bathroom. He was a big, heavily-built man, a contrast to the youth. There was a confused passage then, minutes of soundless dialogue. The woman was weeping, the men at a loss.

Mrs Jaraby sat still, watching carefully. She worked the play out in her mind, relating character to character. The youth put on his overcoat, the man his jacket, the woman was still in a macintosh. There wasn't much action in this play. She preferred it when cars were used, when the camera moved from one place to another. She felt that a climax was approaching, but she knew it wouldn't be very exciting.

She heard her husband in the house; his footsteps on the stairs; his slow movements in the bedroom above. When she listened again there was silence and the rain had stopped.

26

'I paid five hundred pounds to a man called Swingler that he would hush the thing up. It was wasted money, for already the business is public property. Can one trust no one?'

'You are a foolish old man,' said Mrs Jaraby. 'Surely you know that we must take our medicine? Five hundred pounds? You won't see that again.'

'It was my only hope.'

'We are bystanders now. Haven't I said that to you before? We cannot move events or change the course already set. We are at the receiving end now. Our son may call the tune and we must dance. It is only fair.'

'It is not only fair. It is not fair at all. I am not finished yet, no matter what you say. They shall think the better of it and rescind that decision. I shall receive a letter.'

'You shall receive no letter. As to being fair – well, we have had our period. Turn and turn about, you know.'

'That is sheer fallacy. You have lost the capacity for thought.'

'How pleasant that would be. No, I see things clearly still. I envy you your comforting confusion.'

'They will write a letter. Even now they are thinking the better of it. Sanctuary resigned at the injustice.'

'Who knows, you may even get your money back! The man may have a conscience and come with it tomorrow morning.'

'It will rain all day. The heat has broken.'

'The man can cope with rain. He is probably equipped with waterproof coats and wellingtons. Or do you mean that the new season brings fresh hope? Shall you mount a rearguard action this autumn, is that it?'

'I am weary of your provocations. I am provoked enough as it is. The maniac Nox, those silent sheep around the table. Only Sanctuary had courage.'

'Do not seek solace where there is no cause for it. Your public life has failed you too. You must weep if there are tears left with you, and keep your strength for years of slow time ahead. The man has been to see the birds. They will die, he says, one by one.'

'I rejoice in that, as you did when my cat was gone.'

'I killed your cat; you killed my son. The coloured things shall die around us, until the last one drops and we are again alone in this house, you and I, like animals of prey turned in on one another.'

'If you have nothing better to say, may we have peace?'

'Your friend Mr Dowse would turn in his grave to see you cast aside like this, in this ironic way. And how would faithful Monmouth mew now? No, I have nothing better to say. From now on you shall hear me only repeat myself.'

He did not speak. His eyes were open, but were sightless in their stare. She did not knit; she saw no point in knitting now. Basil would not return a second time; the house was a luckless place for him.

'We are left to continue as we have continued; as the days fall by, to lose our faith in the advent of an early coffin. But we must not lose heart: let us think of some final effort. Shall we do something unusual to show our spirit, something we do not often do? You must play a drum in Crimea Road, or walk from the shops bearing kegs of Australian honey. Shall we take breakfast at noon somewhere in public, off the poisoned birds? And shall we march along the streets, talking and laughing, scattering feathers in our path? Do not be downcast; we must not mourn. Has hell begun, is that it? Well, then, I must extend a welcome from my unimportant corner of that same place. We are together again, Mr Jaraby; this is an occasion for celebration, and you must do the talking for a while. Cast gloom aside, and let us see how best to make the gesture. Come now, how shall we prove we are not dead?'